CURIOSITY
KILLED
THE CAT

T.H. HUNTER

CURIOSITY KILLED THE CAT is the first book in the COZY
CONUNDRUMS series.

CONTENTS

Receive Your Free Cozy Conundrums Novella

To sign up for my free mailing list and receive your free novella, THE COCKTAIL CONUNDRUM, please visit *writingmysteries.com*. The novella is part 1.5 in the series and is exclusive to subscribers. You can opt out at any time.

CHAPTER 1

Michelle Nosworthy put aside her notebook, rubbing her tired eyes in determination. She'd show that smug old fart from the *Cotswold Courier* just how much of a mistake it had been to fire her. And just a few weeks before Christmas at that. Once she broke this story, he'd be begging her to return. A proposition she'd reject, of course, but only after watching him squirm for a while. Yes, she'd let his blunder sink in slowly. After this affair was through, major newspapers worldwide would be throwing offers at her. Even a Pulitzer prize for investigative reporting wasn't beyond the realm of possibility.

It would have to wait a few more days, however. Michelle Nosworthy wanted to get everything just right. She had already made a big announcement on her blog and on twitter. The people were waiting. And soon enough, the little town of Fickleton would be swarming with journalists, all trying to get a piece of the pie while it was hot. But only *she* would be able to provide all the juicy details that the public craved to know. They had all been recorded in her trusty notebook that she held in her hands at this very moment.

Drunken laughter and the tinkling of glasses told her that the pub downstairs was already crowded. She checked her phone for the time. It was dead. Strange. She could have sworn it had been at half battery just a while ago. She must have been working longer than she had thought. Luckily, the room provided a digital alarm clock at the side of her bed. She got up and moved the bottle of water in front of it in order to read the time. It was 10.30 pm. She'd better make a fresh start in the morning.

She went into the bathroom and splashed a little water

in her face. It had been a tough day. She was just about to brush her teeth when she suddenly heard a scraping noise at the door. She stopped, listening intently. A moment passed. Perhaps it was the landlord snooping around again. She'd caught him in her room before, though she didn't believe his feeble excuse that he had seen a man enter it for a second. Of course, there had been nobody else there.

Ears pricked, she waited another few seconds. Then, she carefully tiptoed out of the bathroom and over to the door, putting her right eye to the spyhole. The singular fluorescent lamp in the hallway flickered. She looked as far as she could to the left and then to the right, but the corridor was empty. She must have been imagining things. Getting paranoid.

There was every reason to be paranoid, of course. She'd be making a lot of enemies once this affair was made public. That was why she wanted to be out of town when it happened. Her nerves were obviously strained.

She bolted the door and fastened the heavy chain just to be sure. A good night's sleep would do the trick. She could always find a different place to stay at if things got out of hand. She walked back into the bathroom and picked up her toothbrush again.

Then, the lights went out. Judging from the cries and yells below, they had also gone out in the pub. She stepped back into the room, her heart pumping fast. This was just a normal power outage, nothing to worry about. She was being silly. Or was she?

In the darkness, she heard scratching sounds. But this time, they were followed by the unmistakable rustling of metal rings. Her breathing shallow, she grabbed blindly for the bottle of mineral water next to her bed, knocking over the alarm clock as she did so.

Her eyes were slowly adapting to the dark. Somehow – impossibly – the door was being unlocked from the outside. The metal chain was loosening. She was rooted to the spot, frozen by terror. The door was slowly creaking open now. She wanted to scream, but no sound would come out of her mouth as a dark figure stepped into the room.

CHAPTER 2

When Val and I exited the terminal building of Bristol airport on a chilly December morning, only a few cars were parked outside. The freezing cold was pinching my cheeks, so I drew up my coat for warmth. My best friend Val, however, was shaking more from the flight than anything else. And the coffee she was holding was teetering dangerously in her hand as a result.

"Val, careful, you're going to…" I said.

"What?" Val said.

But it was too late. The extra large tumbler went flying through the air. In a desperate attempt to break its fall, Val stuck out her right leg. She twirled on the spot in an awkward pirouette before ending up in a half split. The hot brown liquid, however, spilt all over the pavement, as well as her shoes.

"This was a new pair! Coffee all over them," she said, straightening up with some trouble.

"I'm sorry, Val," I said, trying hard not to laugh. "We'll try to get the stains out as soon as we get there. Here, let me get the tumbler."

"I'm so clumsy," she said miserably. "I just can't seem to get through a day without something happening to me. And spilling coffee is a *very* bad start."

"I think that's our taxi over there," I said, trying to steer the conversation away from anything to do with caffeine. Val believed it was the solution to everything. And so the loss of it was naturally a disaster of existential proportions.

"How far do we have to go, anyway?" she asked, trying to rub off the dark stains from her right shoe with a handkerchief.

"Well, one and a half hours, according to google," I said,

checking my phone again.

"So, that's going to be how many thousands of pounds?" she asked. "I'm on a strict budget, Amy. Waitressing doesn't pay too well, you know. I can't blow it all on a trip through the English countryside."

"You're telling me," I said, rolling my eyes.

I wasn't looking forward to getting back to it myself. My boss had made it his hobby to give me a hard time, but I needed the job. Val and I worked at cafés opposite each other. A few years ago, we had bonded during one of our breaks and had been best friends ever since.

"But don't worry," I continued. "The lawyer said it's all paid for in the letter. Accommodation's also been taken care of, apparently. And I'll get you another coffee when we get there. That'll give you some time to recover from the flight. Deal?"

"OK, Amy. Whatever you say," she said, her mood lightening visibly.

An old-fashioned black cab with a yellow sign on the roof came to a halt next to us.

"Hello, Miss Amanda Sheridan?" the driver asked through the open window.

"Hello, yes, that's right," I said. "And this is my best friend Val."

The driver got out of the car. He had an extremely red but jovial face with a shaven head that couldn't quite hide the fact that he was going bald.

"Nice to meet you," he said. "People just call me Tom. Here, let me take your bags for you."

"No, it's fine, really," I began.

"Don't worry. My pleasure."

We thanked him and got into the backseat. Tom followed shortly, slamming down the hatch and getting into the driver's seat.

"Fickleton House, isn't it? We'll get you there in no time," he said, patting the dashboard affectionately. "She's taken me all over the country, she has. Brought her with me from London. They don't make them like this anymore. Not around here, anyway. All posh silver Mercedes types, but no soul to them. Real beauty, isn't she? Suits the landscape, you could say."

Val looked out of the window, frowning. We had just entered the motorway and were surrounded by nothing but lifeless concrete and asphalt, shrouded in a grey fog that prevented us from seeing anything more than the closest couple of cars. Tom, who had seen her expression in the rear mirror, gave off a throaty laugh, no doubt the result of many pints of beer and packets of cigarettes.

"Oh, jus' you wait, the Cotswolds are beautiful. And that's coming from a man who's only got one eye."

"You've only got one eye, how come?" Val asked curiously. "I hope it wasn't one of your customers."

"No, no, nothing like that," he said, grinning. "More the artsy type of people live around here, if you get my meaning. Rich folk from the cities, music stars, artists. There's going to be a fair in a few days, in fact."

"In Fickleton?" I asked.

"That's right," he said. "Sir Henry is the official host, though everybody knows Lady Worthington is really running the show."

He hesitated briefly.

"Anyway. You here on business?" he asked casually.

"You could say that, yeah," I said. "The thing is… we don't really know ourselves."

"Well, I always enjoy a good mystery," said Tom.

***

We drove on the motorway for quite a while until we reached a junction. Before long, Tom was proven right about the landscape. The sun had found its way through the thick clouds by now, and the fields of yellow and green were shrouded in a dreamy mist as if covered by cotton candy. Most trees had long since shed their leaves, yet some of them still lay at the trunks in faded gold and red.

"Almost there, ladies," Tom said finally. "We're approaching the village now. Very pretty in winter time."

The village of Fickleton was tucked into a small valley between hilly woodlands on either side. An old stone bridge marked the physical threshold beyond which dozens of small houses hugged the narrow main road. On our left, a middle-aged man in a mackintosh was walking his dog, a puppy black Labrador, though nobody else seemed to be out in this weather.

"Fickleton House is on our right, up the hill through the little wood," Tom informed us. "You'll be able to see it soon."

As we turned the first corner a few yards into the village, a dozen or so cars were blocking the road ahead. Some of them, I noticed, were police. Tom rolled down his window, and a young officer approached the car.

"What's going on?" Tom asked.

"Spot of trouble at the pub," the officer said. "May I ask where you're heading?"

"Fickleton House," Tom said, with a slight note of impatience in his voice.

"Sorry, that won't be possible at the moment, sir. We're stopping all cars passing through."

"What happened exactly?" I asked from the back.

"There's been a death. I'm afraid you'll have to get out here."

"Can I at least park the cab at the back of pub – in the car park?" Tom asked in a disgruntled tone. "I live there, you know. That's where I always park."

"I'm afraid the car park is reserved for police only at the moment, sir," the young officer said. "You will have to exit your vehicle here. PC Bowler will be with you in a minute. He's just finishing an interview as we speak."

We had no choice but to comply. A chilly breeze rudely greeted us as we opened the doors of the cab. It seemed other travellers had been stopped before us. A burly policeman with a heavy moustache, undoubtedly PC Bowler, was pompously interrogating an old lady beneath a sign that read "The Mangy Dog". They really loved their quirky pub names around here.

"Sorry for the trouble, ladies," Tom said, as he closed his door. "This could take a while. If PC Bowler is in charge, he's going to make a meal out of it. Probably going to stop every car he can for the next week. Fickleton House isn't too far away, though, just up the hill to your left at the next junction. D'you want me to help with your bags?"

Before Val could say anything, I hastily interjected:

"We'll find our way. Thanks again for the ride."

"No trouble at all. Hopefully see you around in the village some time, eh?"

When we were out of earshot, Val immediately started protesting.

"Why didn't you let him, Amy? These bags are heavy as…"

"Val, he's not your personal chauffeur. It's not his fault we had to stop. We're not even paying the fare. Come on, the walk will do us some good."

We were just about to cross to the other side of the street when the burly policeman with the moustache stopped us.

"And where do you think you're going?" he demanded, puffing up his chest self-importantly. "I'm Police Constable Bowler, and you're trespassing at a potential crime scene."

"We're tourists," Val said immediately. She always had been nervous around law enforcement for some reason.

"Tourists, eh? At this time of year?"

"Well, not so unusual for the Christmas season, is it?" I said. "Anyway, we're also here for another reason. We've got an invitation to Fickleton House, from my great-aunt's lawyer."

He looked at us for a moment with suspicion.

"Names?"

"Amanda Sheridan, and this is Valerie Morgan."

PC Bowler's jaw dropped.

"Amanda Sheridan… are you sure?"

"Of course I'm sure," I said. "It's my name. You don't forget it. Well, not usually anyway."

"Now, now, none of that lip, Missy. You don't know what you're mixed up in here."

"Excuse me? I'm not anyone's 'Missy'," I said hotly. "And I'm not mixed up in anything, either. We just arrived at the airport."

"Might I remind you that this is serious business. There's been a death," he said.

"Who died?" Val asked.

He studied us both in his pompous manner, his small, watery eyes almost disappearing under his bushy eyebrows.

"I suppose it will be in the papers soon enough anyway, so you may as well hear it from an official source. One Michelle Nosworthy, journalist. How long have you been in contact with her, Miss Sheridan?"

"What are you talking about?" I asked.

"I asked you how long you have known the deceased."

"Look," I said in exasperation, "I've never even heard of her until just now. I told you that we only just arrived this morning by plane."

PC Bowler snorted in disbelief.

"We'll be checking up on that little story of yours, Miss Sheridan."

"It happens to be the truth," I said angrily.

"We don't even know what's going on," Val said, rushing to my defence.

"It's none of your business. At least," he said nastily, turning to me, "*not yet*. We found your name in her diary, along with some others. We're still looking for the deceased's notebook, however."

"What?" I asked, totally taken aback. "My name was in…?"

"I'll need the address you're staying at," he continued, interrupting me. "I might have a few more questions after the coroner's report. And once we find her notebook. That's where she kept most of her delicate information. It's bound to turn up sooner or later. Oh, and if I were you, Miss Sheridan, I wouldn't leave the village anytime soon. Some people might get the impression that you have something to hide."

CHAPTER 3

I was still fuming from my encounter with PC Bowler as Val and I made our way through the village and up the hill towards Fickleton House. The bags were heavy, and although both of us were used to a lot of rushing about from waitressing, lugging them uphill had us both panting and out of breath in no time.

"And you really don't know her?" Val asked me for what felt like the hundredth time.

"Don't you start as well, Val. I'm telling you, I've never even heard of her. There must be some mix up. That stupid policeman is just looking for a scapegoat. And who better than some outsider?"

"Yes, but your name was in the diary, though," Val said, puzzled.

"It must be a coincidence," I said. "I can't be the only person in the world with that name. Perhaps there's another Amanda Sheridan around here somewhere."

Val gave me a doubtful look.

"It's unlikely, I know," I said irritably. "But what other explanation is there?"

We had left the village of Fickleton by now and found ourselves on a narrow road, just enough for a car to pass along. The twigs and leaves above our heads covered most of the tentative rays of sunlight that had managed to pass the clouds above, so that it was surprisingly dark for this time of day. The trees formed a natural archway, though they had evidently been trimmed by human hands somewhat.

Finally, the steep slope flattened out before us. Thick hedges flanked old wrought-iron gates, painted black, on either side. The mist was still too thick to see any buildings beyond, though the proud sign to the left of the gate informed us that we had arrived at Fickleton House.

"It's absolutely beautiful," Val said, touching the gates. "Your great-aunt lived here?"

"I don't know. The lawyer's letter was pretty mysterious. Didn't say anything really except that she had died and that my presence was urgently requested."

We passed through the gate and closed it. A long gravel road led straight ahead. Then, in the distance, as the mist gradually receded, I saw the most beautiful place I had ever laid eyes upon. It looked like a manor house, though mimicking a castle in almost every other way. The enormous bowfront with its large oak doors resembled the main gates of a fortress, while the spirals at either side of the house's front mirrored the towers.

Admittedly, the dilapidated condition indicated that its heyday must have been well in the past. Although the grounds were kept neat and orderly, the outer walls were discoloured, with the old paint peeling off in various places. Several windows were broken, and water had undoubtedly penetrated the slate roof, which was lacking tiles almost everywhere.

We approached the doors. There was no bell, so we used the large knocker in the form of a hideous gargoyle instead. We stood there for a while, waiting. Val gazed at the gargoyle, totally mesmerised.

"Maybe this wasn't such a good idea, after all," Val said, looking at me nervously. "This place is creepy, Amy."

I wasn't feeling too comfortable myself.

"Let's just find out what the lawyer wants. Then we can get out of here," I said.

The front door opened with a mighty creak, as though it hadn't done so in a very long time.

An elderly woman with grey-white hair and an old-fashioned, knitted pullover stood there. She looked kind, though suspicious at the same time.

"Yes?"

"Hello, we're here to see Mrs. Sharpe, the lawyer…"

"Ah, yes, of course. We have been expecting you, Miss Sheridan. I am Mrs. Faversham. Please come in."

As we entered, Val suddenly caught her heel on the old rug in the entrance hall and stumbled forward. Luckily, this time, I was able to catch her just in time before she crashed into Mrs. Faversham.

"Thanks, Amy. Close one," Val said, and smiled apologetically at Mrs. Faversham.

The latter looked her up and down with an eagle eye. I could tell that she hadn't quite made up her mind whether to disapprove of us or not.

The entrance hall was dark and cold, though much cleaner than the exterior. Someone was doing their best to keep the house going. We were led past what seemed like an endless number of corridors and closed wooden doors until we reached a hall with a rickety staircase. A slender black cat was perched on the balustrade. Its green eyes, more luminous due to the surrounding darkness, followed our every step, though its body remained perfectly still.

We didn't ascend the stairs, however, as Mrs. Faversham took a left into yet another corridor.

"This place is huge," Val whispered to me.

"Yeah," I agreed.

"You know, if someone tried to murder us in here, they'd never be able to find us," she said.

"I think we can handle Mrs. Faversham," I whispered, grinning. "Though she might try to kill you if you slip on another Persian rug."

We entered a high-ceilinged room with wood panelling, with windows overlooking an inner courtyard. It must have been at the other end of the house because I hadn't seen it as we had approached it. The room we were in sported several paintings – portraits mostly – as well as a large fireplace at the far end. In the middle of the room, there was a long dining table with a three-pronged candle holder. The candles had been lit, as the light from outside wasn't enough to illuminate the place fully.

"Mrs. Sharpe will be with you shortly," Mrs. Faversham said curtly. "Please wait here. I'll light up the fire in a minute."

She exited the room at the other end.

The minutes passed by in silence. I decided to have a closer look at the pictures. The portraits were all of members of the Barrington family, nobles who, judging by the dates, had lived here for hundreds of years. They even had a portrait made of a black cat, quite similar to the one we had seen earlier, though the date said 1959. Perhaps it was the cat's great-grandfather or something.

Meanwhile, Val was trying to get a signal with her phone, just in case of an emergency.

"It's useless," she said. "Like something's jamming the signal."

"You're getting paranoid, Val. Nobody's jamming the signal. Probably just a bad connection. Not surprising out here in the sticks."

"I had three bars outside in the woods, and none on the lawn in front of the house or in here," she said.

"OK. You're right, Val. It's probably a plot to kill a couple of waitresses."

"Oh stop, Amy," she said, though she cheered up a little after that.

Finally, there was a knock on the door.

"Erm, yes?" I said, clearing my throat.

A woman of about forty, wearing a grey two-piece suit and her hair in a bun, entered.

"I am Mrs. Sharpe," she said, stretching out her hand to me and then Val. "How do you do?"

After the introductions, we sat down at the long dining table. Mrs. Sharpe placed her black briefcase on the chair next to her, producing a stack of papers from it.

"Now then, Miss Sheridan. As I stated in my letter to you, your great-aunt passed away several months ago. I have been charged with settling all matters connected to her estate. Tracking you down was quite difficult, and I am glad that you came all this way. I realise that my letter was rather... vague. It was, however, expressly stipulated in the will of your late great-aunt that it was to be so. I understand that you hadn't known her?"

"No, I didn't," I said. "I didn't even know I had a great-aunt."

Mrs. Sharpe shifted a little in her chair.

"I have been her lawyer for almost fifteen years now. It would be something of an understatement to say that she could be a little eccentric at times. She certainly was very particular in regard to how this entire affair was to be treated. And I will do the best I can to accommodate all of her wishes."

She leafed through the stack of papers next to her, producing a single sheet with a long list on it.

"This is a comprehensive list of the items that are bequeathed to you, Miss Sheridan. In addition," she said, taking out two more pieces of paper, "you will inherit this house and the grounds surrounding it, as well as a lump sum as detailed here."

She indicated the third paper and handed it to me. I moved it between Val and myself, so that we could both look at it at the same time. Val and I didn't have any secrets, and I wasn't starting now.

Val saw it first. She inhaled sharply, putting her hand to her mouth. I scanned the page quickly, trying to follow her gaze. At the very bottom, underlined, was the sum I was to inherit. It was just over seven million pounds sterling.

It was like I had been hit by a truck. The rest of the conversation was like a blur to me. Mrs. Faversham came in briefly to set up the fire. Then, I signed papers, answered questions, filled in forms and discussed every little detail until Mrs. Sharpe had worked through the entire stack of papers beside her. It was like some sort of dream. I was tremendously glad that Val was there with me.

Finally, after everything else had been settled, Mrs. Sharpe got up and shook my hand. It was already dark outside.

"Good luck, Miss Sheridan. Oh, before I forget," she said. "I can handle the rest for you from now on, if you wish to keep me as your legal counsel, that is."

"Oh, yes, of course. Thank you," I said, still feeling dazed.

"Excellent," Mrs. Sharpe said, smiling for the first time during our encounter. "There's also the matter of the housekeeper, Mrs. Faversham. You are, of course, free to hire whom you please, though I understand that she has a very great fondness for the house and has loyally served your great-aunt for many years. She is preparing your rooms for the night as we speak, in fact. If there's anything else you'd like to know, don't hesitate to get in touch with me."

She handed me a business card and exited the way she had entered a few hours earlier.

For the first time ever perhaps, both Val and I didn't know what to say to each other.

"Everything's going to change now, isn't it?" I said, still stunned.

"Yep," said Val, grinning. "You're loaded now."

"No more waitressing," I said.

"Nope. Not for you, anyway. Seems like I'll have to look for someone else to spend my breaks with."

"Oh, don't be stupid, Val."

"What?"

"Stay here, with me," I said.

"Sure, I still have an entire week off," she said. "We could do this room up in that time or just…"

"You know what I mean, Val. Permanently."

She looked at me and then out of the window. She had a

peculiar look on her face, but then shook her head.

"Amy, I can't. I mean, it's not like I'm longing to get back or anything but… it's *your* house. I wouldn't know what to do. I can't just live off your money forever. I've always earned my own way."

"But don't you see? It's the same for me, too. I had to fend for myself since I was sixteen, since the day my parents died. I did every job I could get my hands on just to keep afloat. College was always just a pipe dream. And now… now this happened."

I stared at the roaring fire in the fireplace as the truth of the situation gradually settled in. This whole affair would mean an end to my waitressing days. No more washing tables. No more long hours at the till. And best of all, no more bosses. This was a financial freedom I hadn't known in my entire life.

But I was frightened as well. I might not have enjoyed everything about my job, least of all my boss, but I had prided myself on hard work, just like Val. The struggle had kept me sharp and alive. Above all, it had provided meaning. A meaning that would have to be replaced now.

"I need you, Val," I said. "You're like a sister to me. And this whole thing could've just as well happened to you. I got lucky, that's all. That's the only difference. And I can't end up an old spinster in this place all alone."

"Well, with your pickiness about men, I don't know whether I can prevent that," she said, laughing. "So, you want to keep the house?"

"Yeah, I think so. The countryside around here is amazing. And this place will be, too, once we've had a go at it. Anyway, I've got to stay here until PC Bowler is convinced I'm not mixed up in that death at the pub down in the village."

We sat there in silence. She stared into the flames in the fireplace for a while, evidently thinking through my proposition.

Finally she turned back to me and said:

"OK, Amy. Let's restore Fickleton House to its former glory. But I'm getting a job in town somewhere. I want to pay my way."

We hugged. She really was the best friend anyone could hope for. What would I ever do without her?

***

Later that evening, after a makeshift supper that consisted mainly of late coffees and biscuits, Mrs. Faversham led us up to our bedrooms, both of which were very spacious. Apparently, there wasn't any kind of modern equipment in the entire house, not even a telephone. According to Mrs. Faversham, my late great-aunt had disapproved of any kind of electricity, though she had reluctantly tolerated its installation in the small house that Mrs. Faversham occupied, which was located beyond the gardens but still belonged to the Fickleton House estate.

"I worked for your great-aunt for many years, since the end of the war, in fact," she said to me as we entered the bedroom I was to sleep in for the night. "Nice lady, though very private. Kept to herself for the most part. Didn't make her too popular down in the village, I can tell you that. But she was always very decent to me and Charles. Kept me on after he died, as well, kept me busy. Do you have any plans for the house yet?"

She was a very proud old lady, though I could see on her wrinkled face that working here meant a great deal to her. I felt quite uncomfortable in my new role. The most I had ever been in charge of was when I had shown new waiters the ropes at the café. I'd never been a real boss, let alone an employer of domestic staff.

"This was all very sudden," I said. "I'll need some time to adapt. But I… erm… want to keep everything just as it was, Mrs. Faversham."

Her eyes lit up in delight, though the rest of her body remained as composed as ever.

"It is always gratifying to be needed, Miss Sheridan," she said. "And if you don't mind me saying so, also to see new life in the house."

"Please, I'm not... just call me Amanda."

But Mrs. Faversham, now bustling around the bed, pretended not to have heard my feeble attempts at breaking the relationship as employer and employee. Val, seeing me trying to squirm out of my awkward position, was giggling in the background.

"Your great-aunt always had breakfast at 9 o'clock, Miss Sheridan," Mrs. Faversham said. "I'll prepare for two, shall I?"

I was just about to protest and say that we could make our own when Val quickly interjected with a warning glance in my direction.

"That would be fantastic, Mrs. Faversham. We'd really appreciate that."

"Not at all, not at all," she said happily. "Oh, and there are candles and matches in the sideboard over there. It can get a little spooky at night. The cat likes to roam around a bit, bless him."

And with that, she left the room, carefully closing the door behind her.

When I was sure she was well on her way down the stairs, I said:

"This is ridiculous, Val. I've made thousands of breakfasts at the café. One more isn't going to hurt me," I said.

"Not you, perhaps," Val said, a wise expression on her face.

"Val, I can't have servants. That's totally out of the question."

"You heard her, Amy. Mrs. Faversham's done this all her life. She wants to be needed. Just let her do her thing."

"But I can't just live like some sort of aristocrat," I spluttered, but Val stopped me in my tracks.

"It's not your place to rob Mrs. Faversham of her purpose. If you want to run Fickleton House properly, you'll have to start acting like the owner, not like some embarrassed guest."

There was a brief silence as I absent-mindedly looked out of the large double-glazed windows, processing what Val had said.

"It's all just so sudden," I said. "I don't want this to change who I am, that's all."

"Don't worry, I'll let you know when it does," she said. "Come on, let's get some sleep."

***

Half an hour later, I lay in the massive four-poster bed that Mrs. Faversham had prepared for me. The silk bedsheets were warm and soft to the skin. Quite a change from the cheap ones I was used to. My mind was still spinning from the occurrences of the day, though the rotations were getting slower. I was becoming drowsy, my eyelids felt heavy.

Yet the strange sounds in Fickleton House didn't let me sleep for long. The wind ominously whistled through the dark corridors. And I just couldn't shake the feeling that there was another presence in the house. The floorboards right outside in the landing beyond my door creaked, as though someone was walking along them. I was being silly. Surely it was Val going to the bathroom or something.

Unable to fall asleep again, I decided to get some fresh air into the room. I checked my phone on the nightstand. It was 2.30 am. The batteries, however, were almost empty. I had better get some other source of light.

I stepped over to the sideboard and fumbled for the candles and matches. I lit one of them and walked over to the windows behind the bed. I was just about to open one of them when, at the opposite side of the house, across the inner courtyard, I saw a light burning in one of the rooms.

My hair at the back of my neck stood on end. It was unlikely to be Mrs. Faversham. She lived in her own small cottage on the estate grounds, after all. Or had she perhaps left a few candles burning there? Surely, Val wouldn't go wandering around the house alone at this hour.

I slipped out of my room and tip-toed over to Val's room a few doors down the corridor. A candle was burning on the table next to her bed, but she wasn't in it.

My breathing faster and shallower now, I turned back into the corridor.

"Val?"

There was no answer.

I tried to steady myself. No burglar would leave a light burning like that in some remote part of Fickleton House. Perhaps it was Val after all. Maybe she had a good reason to be there, though for the life of me I couldn't think of one.

I briefly thought about calling the police, though with the connection down in these parts, I'd have to walk over to Mrs. Faversham's house for the telephone. I made a mental note of having a phone installed first thing in the morning.

Then, I remembered what Val had told me about acting like the owner of the house. It was perfectly true that I still felt more like a guest in a posh but extremely old-fashioned hotel than anything else. It was time to change that.

I gritted my teeth. Val was right. This was my house now, and I wanted to find out what was going on in it. I grabbed another candle and the box of matches from the sideboard just in case. I peeked through my bedroom window to make sure I hadn't been imagining things. Yes, the light was still burning. If I took a right turn in the next corridor and kept right – with the inner courtyard in view – I should be able to get there without losing my way.

I took out a scrap of paper from my handbag, scribbling a note for Val just in case and placed it on her bed. That way, she'd know where I was. Then, I stepped out into the corridor again.

Though it was still a little cloudy, the moonlight from outside was shining in somewhat. My eyes were gradually adapting to the darkness, too.

I stepped through the empty corridors for quite some time. To avoid getting lost, I looked out for windows, so that I could check my relative position to the courtyard and the room with the burning light. Luckily, I was still on track.

Before long, I reached the corridor I was sure the light was coming from. I checked one of the windows. And there, almost directly opposite, was the candle I had lit in my own room for guidance. I had to be very close now.

I tip-toed forward, trying desperately not to breathe too loudly despite the increasing instinct to do so. And there, near the landing, straight ahead, light was coming through the cracks below the door of one of the rooms. This was it. Whoever it was, they were behind that door.

I carefully extinguished my own light. In case it wasn't Val, I shouldn't advertise my whereabouts. I moved carefully forward, trying to prevent the floorboards from creaking as best I could.

As I stood close to the door, my heart hammering in my chest, I heard a voice through the door. It was undoubtedly male, muttering in some strange language I didn't recognise. The voice was exasperated, almost angry in tone, but then stopped abruptly.

I remained perfectly still, for fear that I had somehow been discovered, holding my hand to my mouth to muffle the sounds of breathing. There was a brief thud. And then, ever so slowly, the door opened from the inside.

CHAPTER 4

Panic-stricken, I watched as the door slowly swung open. I leant against the wall, trying desperately not to be seen. I had nothing to defend myself with. Wildly, I thought of throwing the candles at whoever came out of that door and running for my life during the confusion. A terrible plan, I know, but what else could I do?

As I hid next to the now opening door, the light from within the room shone onto the corridor. And then, a figure stepped in front of the light, so that the shadow stretched out into the corridor. To my horror, it wasn't a man's at all, but some sort of beast, its massive shadow stretching as far as the door's frame would allow. The shadow was coming closer; it was going to step out into the corridor any second now.

But to my bewilderment, nothing emerged from the room until I heard the same voice that had been speaking the strange language.

"Down here," it said.

My eyes tore downward. It was the black cat that I had seen earlier that day on the staircase. It was speaking to me, a look of superior aloofness on its face.

"That's the worst hiding place I've ever seen in my life, by the way. You do realise cats have excellent vision in the dark, don't you?"

"You can speak!" I spluttered.

Was I still dreaming?

"Better than most, I might add," the cat said sniffily. "What are you doing in my house? I do hope you realise that you are breaking and entering."

"*Your* house?" I asked.

"Fickleton House has belonged to my family for

23

centuries. Who are you, pray?"

At that moment, a bloodcurdling call echoed through the corridors.

"Aaaamy?"

It was Val.

"I'm here, Val. It's OK. It's just… just the cat," I called.

That sounded weird but I suppose it was true nonetheless. A few seconds later, Val arrived, totally out of breath and dressed in a pink nightgown.

"I read your message. What's going on, Amy?" she asked.

Still dumbstruck, I just pointed to the cat before us. He simply sighed and said:

"Follow me. I can see this is going to take some time."

Val looked at me as though she were going crazy.

"Amy, did you hear that? The cat spoke… Or did I just have too much cheese? I knew I shouldn't have…"

"Oh, for heaven's sake," the cat said. "Spare me. Now, come on."

We followed him into the room. The most extraordinary sight met my eyes. Thousands of books decorated the walls of the vast room. It wasn't your run-of-the-mill library, however. Every inch of it had been built so that a cat might easily access all areas. Cat stands stretched on all sides to the ceiling. The shelves had ample space for four legs to trod along it. And in the corners, miniature metal hoists had evidently been placed there so that the cat could place the books back on the shelf on his own.

On the floor, dozens of books were scattered around a reading lamp. Various rugs, cushions, and bowls of milk were strewn throughout.

"This is my study," the cat said unnecessarily.

He curled up on one of the cushions and faced us, his black tail moving irritably to and fro. Before he could say anything, Val, still in disbelief, somehow managed to stumble into a table, sending a neatly stacked pile of papers with scrawls of cat claw imprints all over flying into the air.

"Once you've stopped ruining my research, I demand to know what you are doing here," the cat said angrily.

"I might ask you the same thing," I said, as I helped Val up again. "Just so you know, I own this house. Signed everything a couple of hours ago."

The cat scowled at me, swearing under his feline breath.

"Human law may be on your side, though it cannot change the fact that I," he said, stretching out his paw and then placing it on his cat's chest in a majestic fashion, "am the Earl of Barrington. By birthright, Fickleton House belongs to my family. And as the last remaining descendant, to me."

Val, who was still entranced by the contents of the room and had barely been listening, turned to him.

"So what are you researching?" she asked him.

"You wouldn't understand any of it," he said rudely.

"And you are the Earl of … what did you say again?" Val said.

"The Earl of Barrington," he repeated. "You may also address me as 'Your Lordship'."

He was so serious and earnest about it all that both Val and I couldn't supress our laughter fully.

"What?" he said irritably.

"We can't call a cat 'Your Lordship'," said Val.

"We could call him Barry, though, what do you think, Val?" I said, grinning.

"Oh, no, that's absolutely inappropriate for a cat of my…" he began.

"Barry it is, Amy," said Val.

"So, how come you can speak?" I asked him, before he could protest any further.

Barry's whiskers twitched, annoyed at being asked such an impertinent and personal question.

"You say you own the house," he said, ignoring my query. "What is your claim?"

"I inherited it from my great-aunt," I said.

Barry froze. He looked at me as though seeing me for the first time properly. Then, he suddenly let out a furious howl that made Val hold her hands to her ears.

"What's wrong?" I asked.

Barry shook himself, as though trying to expel some sort of demon force that had taken hold of him. Finally, he got up and began pacing around his reading area.

"Barry…" Val said tentatively.

"Not now, I'm thinking," he said. "And don't call me that."

He brooded for a few more minutes. I looked at Val, who simply made shrugging motions with her shoulders. This was bizarre to say the least. We couldn't have both gone crazy. And yet, here we were, talking to a black cat with an ego the size of the entire estate.

Finally, Barry turned to me and said:

"Yes. Only one way to find out."

He moved over to the bookshelf at the far end of the room. Squeezed between several books was a small cardboard box, which Barry pulled out with some trouble. He took it in his mouth and trotted back to us again.

"Open it," he said to me after he had plonked it in front of my feet.

I bent down and lifted the lid off from the thin cardboard container. Within was a beautifully carved wooden stick. It had a grip that was thicker than the rest of the wood, which made it feel natural and effortless to hold in my right hand.

"What is it?" I asked Barry.

"It's a wand, of course. My wand, in fact. So treat it with the uttermost care. Go on, give it a wave," Barry said, his whiskers twitching slightly.

I felt silly doing so, but I was also curious about where this was all going to lead. Val, who seemed to be taking the whole thing a lot more seriously now, nodded to me.

Lifting the wand high above my head, I brought it down with a swoosh through the air. To my utter amazement, little red sparks bubbled out of the tip, leaving a trail of crimson in its wake. Val clapped loudly, while Barry wore a look of satisfaction.

"I knew it," he said. "I can always tell."

"What do you mean?" I asked.

"You are a witch," he said.

"I beg your pardon?" I asked.

He sighed.

"You can do magic," he said.

"What?"

"That's the definition of being a witch," he said.

"But that's just not …" I began, but he interrupted me immediately.

"Didn't you pay any attention?" he said.

Then, still staring into my disbelieving face, he strutted over to one of the books lying on the floor. It was a massive old tome with mysterious symbols etched onto the spine and cover. He opened it and flicked through the pages as we edged closer. The chapter titles ranged from "Useful Everyday Cooking Spells" to "Rules and Regulations for Witches and Warlocks".

"What are you doing?" Val asked him.

"I'm looking for the fastest way to get this cumbersome conversation over with. So I need a spell that's simple yet convincing. Ah yes, this is pretty basic. You should be able to do this without too much practice."

He had placed his paw on a chapter entitled "Water spells – Basic Beginnings". Each spell had a name, a description, as well as a hand-drawn sketch of the wand movements for correct usage.

"Try the first one," Barry said.

"Go on, Amy," said Val, eager to see more magic.

Keeping my eye on the page to follow the instructions, I waved the wand with a downward flick and said:

"Aqua."

A torrent of water shot out of the tip of my wand, drenching Barry from head to paw.

"Don't point it at me!" he said angrily, shaking off the water.

"I'm sorry, Barry," I said, hastily pointing the wand out of the window.

Val took one of the rugs and started drying his fur. Barry, his whiskers still drooping from the water, closed his eyes as if it cost him tremendous willpower and concentration not to explode at my dilettante attempts at magic.

"There really should be a license for novice witches," he said. "Absolute safety hazard, the lot of you. But, of course, the *Spellcasters' Association* won't listen to me as usual. Be that as it may, however."

"But how...is this possible?" I asked, turning to Barry.

"Didn't you know who your great-aunt was?"

I shook my head.

"Well, that certainly explains a lot," said Barry, whose hair was now standing on end, making him look like a hedgehog.

"Was my great-aunt a witch, then?" I asked.

"Naturally. Despite her illegitimate claims to this house, I cannot deny that she was one of the best witches out there," said Barry. "Magical powers are inherited, you see. You should be getting a lot of junk mail from those busybodies from the *Association* any day now."

Val and I looked at each other in astonishment. If I hadn't just had proof of what Barry had said, I would have had a hard time believing a word of it. Good thing he had started with the demonstration first.

"Now that I have helped you," Barry continued, "I want you to help me in return. I want you to help me transform back into a warlock."

"You're a ... a warlock?" I asked.

"Yes, yes. Now, what you'll have to do is…"

"How did you turn into a cat, then?" asked Val, unable to help herself.

Even the mere memory of it seemed to be extremely painful to him.

"I am an experimental warlock," he said, indicating the many books and papers on the floor beside him with his paw. "One of the best, if I say so myself. Even the buffoons at the *Spellcasters' Association* don't deny it. I invent new spells and refine old ones. I was close to a breakthrough in therianthropy when this happened."

"Theri… what?" asked Val.

"Shapeshifting into animals in layman's terms. Unfortunately – with no fault of my own, of course – one of my spells turned permanent. Too powerful, too much magical power behind it. I've been working ever since to get back into my human shape."

"How long have you been a cat, then?" I asked.

"Over fifty years," he said with a stony face.

Val and I looked shocked.

"Poor Barry," Val said. "That's awful!"

"Yes, yes. Trapped in this furry body for half a century. All very tragic. Now can we get on with it? Because I'd rather not spend the next fifty years chit-chatting."

I nodded, wand at the ready. He waded through his stack of papers with his paws. After a while, he had found what he had been looking for and grabbed it with his mouth. He placed it in front of me on the ground.

"I've marked all of the required wand movements," he said. "Make sure you follow them to a 't', otherwise it won't work."

I bent down and picked it up. From Barry's rough sketches, which were not bad at all considering he presumably had to hold the pencils with his cat paws, were extremely complicated.

I pointed my wand at Barry, who was torn between

flinching with dread at a novice witch pointing a wand at him and the pleasant possibility of turning back into a warlock again. Torn between hope and dread, he kept one eye tightly shut and the other open.

"Mutato in incantatorem!"

Nothing happened.

***

Barry insisted that I try again. And again after that. We stuck at it for I don't know how long. The sun was already rising outside. Val, finally bored of watching the same failed magic over and over again, had been reading a book called *Magic to Mastery: A Beginner's Guide* for the last hour or so.

Finally, Barry cursed loudly and just slumped down on the floor, utterly shattered.

"Shall I do it again?" I asked, exhausted.

"No, there's no point. There was only a remote possibility anyway. Even your great-aunt couldn't do it."

"Couldn't you do it yourself?"

"My magical powers are greatly diminished as a cat. Can't even hold the blasted wand properly," Barry said. "Barely enough to light a candle."

Suddenly, he looked forlorn like a lost kitten. I didn't know whether warlocks-turned-cats could cry, but he certainly looked close to tears. Beneath that veneer of cynicism and superiority lay something vulnerable and fragile. I bent down to him and gently stroked his fur. It seemed to calm him a little.

"It's almost 9 o'clock, Amy," Val said, checking her watch. "We'd better get down to the dining room soon. And I need to freshen up a bit."

"Do you want to have something, Barry?" I asked him.

Barry, all self-pity now, nodded his little head.

"Yes, a little something might cheer me up. I've been working so hard lately."

***

Downstairs, Mrs. Faversham had really outdone herself. Two full English breakfasts were waiting for us, as well as tea, juice, and coffee. There was even a bowl of cat food and some milk for Barry on the floor.

"I do hope it's alright with you, Miss Sheridan, it's only that your late great-aunt always allowed the cat to eat in the same room with her," Mrs. Faversham said as soon as we had entered the room. "But I can remove him, of course, if you prefer."

I looked at an indignant Barry, who threw a warning glance in my direction.

"Yes, he shouldn't *really* be in here," I began, teasing Barry, who was now making cutting motions with his paw in front of his throat. "But he can stay for now – if he behaves, that is."

"Oh, he certainly will in here," Mrs. Faversham said, oblivious to Val's suppressed laughter and the sour look on Barry's face. "But I have seen him pinch a couple of candles now and then. Naughty little fellow. God only knows what he does with them. Your great-aunt made a very nice spot for him to sleep in the study, you know. She was rather fond of him."

"Yes, I've seen his – I mean, the library he sleeps in," I said. "I think we'll keep it as it is for the moment. Thank you very much for the lovely breakfast, Mrs. Faversham."

"Not at all," she said, beaming. "If there's anything else you'd like, I'll be in the kitchen. It's to your left and down the hall. Just leave everything on the table when you're finished."

After she had left the room, Barry had evidently returned to his normal self again.

"What do you mean *I* can stay," he said. "I was just about to say that I tolerate *your* presence here."

31

"Barry, is that your way of saying you're fond of us already?" Val said, winking at me.

He looked at both of us for a moment, considering whether he should admit to it openly or not.

"I need someone to try out my new spells, after all," he said casually. "Anyway, Amanda, you won't be able to get far with your magical training without me. You're too old to be accepted into a school of magic."

"Hey, I'm not even thirty yet," I said in mock indignation.

"My point is," Barry continued. "You *need* me. You won't be able to perform the bond without my extensive knowledge and experience, either."

"What is the bond?" I asked.

He looked at his paw self-importantly before rubbing it against one of his legs as if wiping off an imaginary stain.

"A witch or warlock may bond with a heb – that's what we call a non-magical person – to allow them access to the magical world."

"I choose Val, of course," I said, without hesitation.

"You'll have to," said Barry. "There are strict secrecy protocols. With the exception of family members, hebs aren't to know about us, unless they are inducted properly within the confines of the bond."

"Can I get powers, too?" Val asked eagerly.

"You won't become a full witch, no," Barry said. "But there are certain supernatural skills you may acquire. It is a complicated process and depends on your natural aptitude."

Val looked rather down in the dumps.

"You'll be our specialist, then, Val," I said, trying to cheer her up.

"So what kind of skills are we talking about?" she asked Barry.

"You won't know until it's done," he said. "But telepathy, mindreading, and increased strength are among the most common."

Val looked a little more cheerful.

Then, there was a knock on the dining room door. I cleared my throat.

"Erm, yes?"

Mrs. Faversham entered once again. This time, however, she was followed by a handsome yet slightly worn-out looking man, a few years older than I was, with untidy dark hair that had been hastily combed back. He was wearing a smart blue suit and a black tie that matched his hair.

"This is Mr. Lavalle," Mrs. Faversham said, eyeing him with suspicion. "He says he'd like to talk to you about the death that happened in the pub down in the village."

"Oh, OK," I said, taken aback. "Please, have seat, Mr. Lavalle. We were just finishing breakfast."

"Thank you," he said with a pleasantly deep voice that resonated off the oak panelling in the room.

After the initial introductions, he hesitated somewhat, evidently waiting for Mrs. Faversham to leave the room. She was standing with arms crossed at the door, still watching him like a hawk.

"It's quite alright, Mrs. Faversham," Val said. "We can deal with it."

"Alright," she said, still not entirely convinced. "As I said, I'll be in the kitchen. Just call when you need me."

With one last look at Mr. Lavalle, she closed the door.

"I must say, you do have quite an inquisitive housekeeper," he said. "Hardly let me in at all."

"You say you're here because of the death in the village?" I said.

"Yes. Now, before I tell you this, I need to know whether you know about... your great-aunt."

Before I could say anything, however, Barry intervened.

"You mean that she was a witch?" Barry said.

"Barry! Didn't you just tell us about keeping it secret?" Val whispered.

"It's alright," Barry said loudly. "I can spot a warlock

from a mile off. Mr. Lavalle is one of us."

The latter looked not at all surprised to see a cat speak.

"Yes, you're quite right," he said to Barry, lowering his voice conspiratorially. "I'm with Magical Law Enforcement – MLE for short. We have a serious problem. Miss Sheridan, I'm afraid the local heb police suspects you of murder."

CHAPTER 5

My mouth fell open. It was one thing being told by PC Bowler not to leave the village. It was quite another to be suspected of such a heinous crime by the investigators.

Barry, however, was all matter of fact and strutted over to the table, nimbly jumping onto it. Val and I were too stunned by the news to protest.

"But that's absurd," I said. "Val and I only arrived by plane yesterday. When we entered the village, the local police were already at the pub. There's no way I could've done it."

"I know," said Mr. Lavalle, sighing heavily. "There have been a string of murders in the Cotswolds. All mysterious circumstances, with no traces of the killer. He's devilishly clever, that's for sure. The hebs are desperate to find the culprit, but of course they never will, bless them."

"And why won't they?" Val asked.

"For the simple reason that the perpetrator is almost certainly a witch or a warlock," he said.

Barry cursed.

"Does that mean the place will be crawling with MLE agents?" Barry asked, obviously annoyed at the prospect.

But Lavalle shook his head, mistaking Barry's tone for desperation.

"No, I'm afraid not. Resources are very thin at the moment. I'm with the London department usually, you see. Most of my colleagues are tied up with a big case of art heist."

"An art heist?" I said.

"Yes," he said. "A series of art heists, to be exact. There is reason to believe that they are connected, however."

"But why would witches or warlocks be interested in

stealing pieces of art?" I asked.

"I think," said Lavalle, rubbing his cheek absent-mindedly, "the question is rather why more sorcerers *don't* do it. You can conjure up cash or befuddle the bank manager, no problem, but a Da Vinci or a Van Gogh will always be unique. A magical copy is just that – a copy."

"Sorcerers is what we call spellcasters who've broken the law," Barry added helpfully.

"Oh, you haven't been a witch for long?" Lavalle asked me, smiling.

"No," I said. "I found out yesterday. From Barry, in fact."

"The Earl of Barrington, that is," Barry corrected me irritably.

"But you can also call him 'Your Lordship'," said Val, affectionately stroking Barry, who was looking daggers at her.

"Oh, I think I've heard of you," said Lavalle enthusiastically. "You were the warlock who couldn't turn himself back, aren't you?"

"You're famous, Barry," I said, grinning.

Barry scowled at all of us.

"You were saying that Amanda is a murder suspect?" he said.

Lavalle's face became serious again.

"That's right. As I said, the hebs are desperate to pin this on someone. And they prefer to do it to an outsider rather than one of the village locals. Less trouble that way."

"Typical," said Barry.

"But that's not fair," said Val, smacking the table with her open hand.

"I agree," Lavalle said. "But it's the ugly truth nevertheless. If they can blame an outsider, they don't have to tread on anyone's toes around here, you see."

"But it's never going to stick," I said. "I can prove that I took that plane."

"Maybe," Lavalle said. "But the heb police are known to have falsified evidence in these cases. The thing is, there's no way they can catch a sorcerer. He or she will always be one step ahead of them. Not a chance. They don't know why, of course. Usually, it just becomes another unsolved cold case, one among many. But this is different. The investigators are under pressure from the local communities and politicians. They must solve it, one way or the other. And they'll resort to a convenient scapegoat if they have to."

"But how can I prevent them from framing me?" I asked, getting more agitated by the minute. "Can't we just… modify their memories or something?"

Lavalle shook his head sadly.

"That's what we usually do if we get ahead of them. But not in this case. It's too public by now. There are thousands, perhaps over a million hebs who know already. You know, through newspapers, internet websites, gossip. We'd never be able to stem the flow of information, even if we weren't understaffed. It's out there for good, I'm afraid."

"But what can we do?" I said.

"There's only one way forward," Lavalle said. "We need to solve the case before the hebs can blame you for it. That's why I've been sent here by the MLE, in fact. Once we've caught the culprit and have enough evidence, we can hand them over to them."

"Won't a sorcerer just escape, though?" Val asked.

"After a fair magical trial, they are stripped of their powers by the *Spellcasters' Association* for the duration of their sentence," Lavalle said.

"Why did they send you specifically?" Barry asked shrewdly.

Lavalle laughed, though there was some bitterness there, too.

"That's anyone's guess. I know the terrain, however, so

37

I assume I was an obvious pick. And most of my colleagues are divided on the subject of the importance of this case."

"What do you mean?" I asked.

"Well, some of my colleagues in London believe it's a random act of murder or a serial killer on the loose. A sorcerer on a spree, if you will. Others disagree, believing it is connected to the art thefts somehow."

"Val, remember what Tom, the taxi driver, told us? There's going to be an arts fair here soon," I said. "I wonder if it's got something to do with the murder that occurred. What do you think, Mr. Lavalle?"

"It could be a coincidence," he said blankly. "And please, just call me Lavalle. Everyone does at the office."

"OK. But not everyone thinks it's a coincidence?" I said.

Lavalle frowned slightly.

"No. My older brother Alec – he's a private investigator in London – fed me some interesting information. He's been undercover for some time now, infiltrating a criminal organisation that he thinks is run by sorcerers. All hearsay and no proof, so his superiors keep telling him, but enough for him to keep digging a little deeper."

"But there's no proof so far?" I asked.

"Not that I am aware of," said Lavalle.

"You mentioned a spree, Lavalle," said Barry. "Who are the victims in the case you're investigating?"

"Well, aside from Michelle Nosworthy, the woman who was murdered in the pub yesterday, there've been two previous murders in the area. Most likely connected. I'll be investigating them in chronological order, as it were, but I just wanted to speak to you first. You see, I need your help, Miss Sheridan."

"Of course, how can I help?"

Lavalle took a deep breath, running a hand through his hair to keep it out of his tanned face.

"I want you to keep out of trouble while I'm out of town. PC Bowler and the heb inspector will grasp at any straws you give them."

I hesitated for a moment as Lavalle got up from his chair.

"So you're basically asking me to just stay put? I thought your department was overstretched as it is."

"Yeah, we could help," said Val.

"I cannot allow you to interfere, Miss Sheridan. You're at great risk as it is. We shouldn't provoke the hebs any further. Or give them any more opportunities to frame you."

"But I can't just sit here and do nothing," I said.

"I'm afraid you'll have to," he said. "I'll get back to you as soon as I can with any new developments. I can find my own way. Goodbye."

And with that, Lavalle let himself out the way he had come. I stared at the closed door for a while, deep in thought.

"Amy, are you OK?" Val asked finally.

I spun around. Barry had returned to his bowl as if the matter had been settled.

"We can't just watch while this sorcerer preys on more innocent victims," I said.

"But Mr. Lavalle specifically said we couldn't intervene," Val said.

"Yes, I know..."

Barry, sensing a dangerous turn of events, tore himself away from his bowl again and leapt back onto the table.

"What you are intending is totally out of the question, Amanda," he said, pointing his paw at me. "There's no point walking around the village, pretending to be a detective. Magical Law Enforcement agents undergo years of training and must have a lot of experience before they may investigate on their own. You have neither. You didn't even know you were a witch until last night."

"You heard him, Barry, his department isn't going to send out any more people, he's on his own," I said hotly.

"The sorcerer who is behind it all means business. And so do the heb policemen. Novice witch or not, I can't just sit idly by while they frame me for murder!"

"Innocent until proven guilty," said Barry.

"Not for them and you know it, Barry," I said angrily.

It would be a way to clear my name. Not only was my freedom on the line, but the guilty party would still be free to continue to roam the countryside. Perhaps even to kill again. And I couldn't deny that the prospect of catching the perpetrator didn't excite me, as well. I could see that I had convinced Val, but Barry looked nervous.

"I'm not getting pulled into a murder case," he said. "I've got research to do. I'm a cat, after all, and there's only so much I can do. Best to keep your head low in these times…"

"Barry, are you afraid of the sorcerer?" Val asked bluntly.

"Afraid? Of course I'm afraid! I can't even hold a wand properly, let alone defend myself against a powerful sorcerer," said Barry, self-justification seeping out of every syllable.

"Neither can I," said Val. "But Amy can, if you help her."

Barry looked at Val and then at me. I could see he was torn. But I also knew that he was a much better person than he liked to pretend.

"Alright, alright, I'll help," he said gruffly. "You'd probably get yourselves killed anyway if you tried any spells on your own."

"Excellent," I said, beaming at Barry.

"Where shall we start?" Val asked.

I pondered the question briefly.

"Well, Lavalle is going to the other two crime scenes, we may as well go down to the pub and see what we can find out. Barry, what do you think?"

"Fine," he said. "But we should do the bond first. We'll

need every advantage we can get."

***

A few minutes later, we found ourselves back in Barry's study again. He was diligently preparing the series of spells I had to cast in order to initiate the bond with Val, who was lying on the floor.

"I feel silly," Val said, as Barry drew a circle around her with a piece of chalk in his mouth.

"Won't be long, Val. I think. Will it, Barry?" I asked.

He had completed the circle and let the chalk drop to the floor.

"An hour, at most," he said. "I haven't done this in many years. I'm somewhat out of practice."

"Ooh, Barry, did you bond with anyone? A heb lady friend, perhaps?"

"Certainly not," he said.

"Wasn't there ever a Lady Barrington?" I asked.

"If ever, her title would have been Countess of Barrington. But no, there wasn't. I was always married to my work."

"Spoken like a true scholar," I said, grinning.

Barry huffily changed the subject.

"We can now proceed with the bond. Amanda, I need you to stand over there at the lectern. The first book we'll need is *Magical Contracts* by E.W. Arcbridge. You'll find it on the shelf behind you."

The procedure involved a series of complicated incantations, many of which I had to repeat over and over again until Barry was satisfied that they had worked. Invariably, after every spell, he'd jump from his place and watch Val very closely for any sign of change, prodding her in the arm or sniffing at her face.

"What are you looking for?" I asked, bewildered. Personally, I couldn't see any difference in Val at all.

"Magic leaves unmistakable traces to the trained eye," he said as he studied her right hand.

In preparation of every spell, Barry either sprinkled strange powders over Val's body or provided foul-smelling liquids for her to drink.

Finally, after the best part of an hour had passed, Barry seemed satisfied. I still couldn't detect any difference in Val, aside perhaps from a disorientation that was more pronounced than usual.

"How do you feel, Val?" I asked.

"Weird."

"Yes, well, I'm sure that was there before we started," said Barry. "Anything more specific?"

"I – I don't know," she said, looking at us as though she were doing so for the first time. "It's only… Barry, are you OK?"

"Of course I am," he said. "Apart from the fact that I'm doomed to spend the rest of my days as a cat, of course."

"I know," Val said.

"What do you mean, 'you know'?" I asked.

"I know how he feels about it – about being a cat forever. And," she continued, looking at me, "I know how you feel, Amy, about being the subject of a murder investigation. I can *feel* it."

"Great," Barry said, rolling his eyes. "She's an empathetic psychic."

"An… empathetic psychic?" Val repeated slowly.

"Yes. We will see how far your abilities reach in the coming months."

"But this is brilliant," I said. "Val, this can help us find the killer! We'll just talk to everyone in the village and you can read their minds, one by one."

Barry tried to wag his finger at me in disagreement, but ended up just waving his paw.

"No, no, no. All human superstitious nonsense. The mind is not like a book full of information you can read at leisure. And luckily so, otherwise you'd be wading through thousands of pages of information. You'd never find anything. Skilled psychics can gain access to *active* pathways, especially if they have a deep emotional meaning."

"But surely, a murder would be emotional." I said.

"In some circumstances, perhaps. But not always. I doubt the average hitman feels very much. And trained witches and warlocks can shield themselves from detection, as well. As I shall be doing, in fact."

"Don't worry, Barry," I said teasingly. "Nobody needs psychic powers to know how you feel about things."

***

It was already getting dark when we stepped out of the house in order to go down to the village pub. I still couldn't believe that the beautiful grounds of Fickleton House were my home for good. It still felt as though I was a visitor to some house that belonged to the National Trust or a time-travelling guest to some 19th century hotel.

The nights were already approaching freezing point, but at least it was a crisp coldness. Val, who was prone to it and had thus always preferred warmer climates, was complaining non-stop until we reached the main street. Barry accompanied us and for once seemed quite contented. He still criticised our plans at every stage, of course, but his curmudgeonly refusal was gradually giving way to something more productive.

The roads remained as sleepy as they had been the previous day. The bus stop was empty, shunned even by the obnoxious youths that usually frequented such places. A few cars were parked outside "The Mangy Dog" as we approached it, though the police had evidently left by now. The pub's little metal sign, featuring a shaggy black dog, was creaking slightly in the light breeze that had followed us down into the valley where the village lay. Through the circular milk glass panes, I could make out a number of figures. It seemed that the pub was pretty busy.

Val and I entered first, with Barry close behind us. Immediately, a cacophony of laughter and loud chatter greeted us. The interior was cosy, with sturdy old furniture and even a fireplace at the back. Most people were deep in conversation, though quite a number peeked their heads to get a closer look at the strange faces that had entered their domain. A staple of village life.

"Not bad. What do you think, Val?" I said.

But Val didn't answer. I turned around and was shocked to see her white in the face, as if she were about to faint.

"Val! What's up?"

"Just too… too many…"

"Let's sit down quickly," Barry hissed from the corner of his mouth.

I took Val by the waist and manoeuvred her to the nearest table. She still looked very pale. Barry, meanwhile, jumped on to the bench next to her.

"Sorry, Amy," Val said after she had steadied somewhat. "Just t-too many feelings floating around. Too many people. My head is buzzing."

"Amanda, you'll have to go to the landlord. I don't know whether he allows me to be here. I'll take care of Valerie," Barry said.

I nodded and went over to the counter. A friendly-looking man with grey hair and a beard greeted me. I asked him if Barry could stay.

"Well," he said, "I don't get cats in here too often. It's dogs mostly."

"He's very well behaved, I assure you. At least, most of the time," I said.

"Oh, that's alright then. I suppose if the sign with the dog outside didn't scare him off, nothing will," he said jovially. "Want a pint?"

Val was big on cider, so I ordered her one, as well as a

bowl of milk for Barry. I got a Guinness for myself.

"I'm surprised so many people are here after the business yesterday," I said as I handed him the money.

"Yes," the landlord said, frowning. "They all want to know what happened. Strange case, you know."

"How come?"

"Well," he began, but hesitated. "Say, are you from around here?"

"I just got here with my friend Val," I said, pointing to our table.

Now it was my turn to pause. I wasn't sure volunteering too much information was the best idea, though in a village of this size, it was only a matter of time before the news spread about the new occupants of Fickleton House. Openness, I finally decided, would probably get me further than caginess.

"I inherited Fickleton House from my great-aunt. Quite unexpected, but there you go. I'm Amanda, by the way."

"Always glad to welcome a new resident, I'm Charles – but people just call me Charlie," he said, relieved. "Thought you might be another reporter. Not that I have anything against reporters, mind you, but Miss Nosworthy – the woman who died – did quite a lot of poking around, you might say."

"D'you think that got her killed?" I asked.

"I'm sure of it," the landlord said, lowering his voice. "I shouldn't really say this, I suppose, but her notebook's missing. That's where she wrote down all the stuff she found out here in the village. I saw her with it every morning. But the police couldn't find any trace of it in her room. Normally, she never left it out of her sight."

"So, you think the killer might have stolen it?"

"Yes. She made a lot of enemies. She had her fair share of arguments with the locals, too, I can tell you that."

"Arguments? With whom?"

"Well," he said uncomfortably. "I wasn't meaning to

eavesdrop, you've got to understand. But the walls are pretty thin at the back where her room was. You know, you just happen to hear a lot when you're in the kitchen, that's all. Talked a lot on the phone with people. Got pretty heated, I reckon. And then, a few days ago, she had an awful row with Lady Worthington at breakfast. In the lounge in the next room."

"Lady Worthington? I think I've heard of her. Isn't she hosting some sort of arts fair?" I asked.

Charlie, the landlord, nodded.

"Not just any old arts fair, at that," he said. "She's got a real Van Gogh painting that's going to be on display. Should attract quite a lot of people to the village."

"So what were they arguing about?" I asked.

"I don't know. The only thing I do know is that Lady Worthington stormed in here – she doesn't normally come to the pub, you have to understand – and blew her top. Just like that. I've seen many rows in my lifetime, but she was downright scary."

After a furtive glance in the direction of the other patrons, he leant in even further to make sure nobody heard us.

"And when Miss Nosworthy refused to stop poking into her affairs, Lady Worthington even threatened to kill her."

CHAPTER 6

Back at the table, I quickly told Val and Barry what had happened. Val, who was still pale in the face from being overwhelmed by her new psychic abilities, looked worried. Despite the initial excitement, I think she hadn't quite warmed up to the idea yet that confronting the murderer would be extremely dangerous as well. I had to say I wasn't too keen on the prospect of facing a homicidal sorcerer myself, though I felt I had little choice given the circumstances.

Barry, however, was deep in thought. I had placed his bowl on the bench next to me. He liked places that were higher up and would provide better vision. I suppose you couldn't be a transformed cat for long without adopting some of the habits of a real one.

"Can you sense anything from the landlord, Val?" I asked.

She shook her head.

"There are just too many people in here. It's all muddled. Maybe if we came back later at some point, when he's alone."

We sipped at our drinks (and bowl of milk) in silence for a while, until Barry stretched his head above the table as far as his feline neck would go, checking whether the coast was clear for him to speak. He needn't have worried, however. The noise from the other tables was so loud with excited chatter and gossip that no one could possibly overhear us.

"We should pay Lady Worthington a little visit tomorrow," he said softly, his eyes still scanning his surroundings.

"Have you heard of her, then?" I asked him.

"Unfortunately yes," Barry said with a haughty

expression. "Arrogant beyond imagination."

"Coming from you, that's saying something," I said, grinning at Barry.

"Yeah, she must be pretty bad," Val agreed.

Barry narrowed his eyes briefly at our jibes, but apparently decided not to dignify them with a response.

"Be that as it may, she's not a *real* aristocrat," he continued, brushing off a splatter of milk from his chest with a stroke of his paw. "Her husband received a knighthood I believe, for a bit of music he composed. Awful, modern stuff. But it doesn't stop her from acting like she's the Queen, of course. Quite the contrary."

"Doesn't sound like she'd be too forthcoming with information," I said.

"Oh, she'll talk," Barry said.

"But what reason would she have to talk to us at all?" I said. "I mean, we can't force her to talk to us, not even to let us in. Especially if she's involved somehow, she's not going to spill the beans to a couple of strangers."

"Amy's right, you know," Val said, still dazedly clutching her head. "We'll be thrown out the minute we get there."

Barry rolled his eyes impatiently.

"Really," he said. "Perhaps it would have been better for you to remain hebs since you insist on thinking like them."

"What do you mean?" asked Val.

"I have a plan," said Barry.

"A plan?"

"Yes. One that involves magic."

***

After finishing our drinks, we made our way back to Fickleton House. Mrs. Faversham was already awaiting us there with a steaming-hot pie, which we gratefully tucked into. Barry remained frustratingly monosyllabic whenever we tried to ask him about his plan to weasel out information from Lady Worthington.

Instead, he skedaddled up to his library as soon as we were all through with dinner, leaving Val and me in a state of bewilderment.

"Oh, he'll come up with something," Val said. "Let's ask him again in the morning."

"I suppose," I said.

"So," said Val, "d'you think it could be Lady Worthington? If the reporter was messing around with her arts fair, that'd be a pretty good motive."

"Yes, that's true. I wonder what made her so mad, though. Lady Worthington, I mean."

"Well, if whatever Barry is planning works, we'll know tomorrow," Val said. "Anyway, I think I'll turn in, Amy. This whole business of being a psychic is pretty... exhausting. I feel a bit ill."

"But you're happy we did it, right?" I asked.

I had somewhat of a guilty conscience. After all, it had been me who had got her into all of this in the first place.

"Yes," she said quickly. "Of course, Amy. I always wanted to know what other people were thinking and feeling. Really."

"Something's bugging you, Val. I don't need to be a psychic to see that."

"It's all just so sudden. And I always enjoyed going out. What if I can never do it again because I'm so overwhelmed by all the different feelings and voices around me? Or have to recover for hours afterwards? You know how much I love partying, Amy. Our monthly cocktail parties at home were legendary."

It was perfectly true, of course. You could always count on Val to go to the next party. Meanwhile, she had to drag me to most of the few I did attend. We both loved cocktail nights, though, for which we'd invite friends over to either Val's or usually my place. Something I was meaning to have a go at in Fickleton House once I got settled in a little more.

"Look, Val," I said, trying to stay on the bright side. "It's early days. You don't know how these things will develop. Perhaps… perhaps there's some sort of technique to close your mind or something. Or a spell. I'm sure Barry knows. Or we could read up on it ourselves in the library. Barry's always boasting about his extensive collection. There must be tons of stuff on the bond and on psychics up there."

"OK," Val said. "Let's do that. Tomorrow. But I want another cocktail party, Amy. It's hard enough giving up on everything else. We could invite some of the locals, get to know them a bit."

"Alright, we'll do that," I said. "First thing after the arts fair, we'll have our cocktail party. I promise."

***

The next day, Val was still feeling very much under the weather, so I brought up her breakfast to her room. She wouldn't be going anywhere anytime soon, so it was up to Barry and me to talk to Lady Worthington.

"Where have you been?" Barry demanded when I finally came back down into the dining room.

"I didn't want Val to eat her breakfast alone, Barry," I said.

"While I am waiting here for you, I might add," he said.

Mrs. Faversham, who knew nothing of Barry's transformation, of course, was nevertheless very fond of him. He received normal cat food only when she couldn't help it. Today, cooked tuna was on the menu, and Barry had gulped it down eagerly.

"Your bowl is empty, Barry," I said.

"Well, you couldn't expect me to eat it cold, could you?"

"Even better," I said, sitting down at the table. "You can tell me about our plan while I tuck in. I'm famished."

He seemed to be racking his brains in search of some

way he could object to this proposal. When he couldn't, he said:

"Fine, Amanda. Always happy to entertain when Valerie isn't here to do it for you."

"Are you jealous, Barry?" I said.

"Me? Jealous?" he said, his whiskers quivering with indignation. "Might I remind you that I have been living here for a long time, virtually on my own? I don't *need* anyone."

"Except Mrs. Faversham and her cooked breakfasts, you mean?"

"Well," he spluttered. "Well, that's different. Entirely beside the point. A working relationship. A warlock's got to eat, you know. Even if he has to spend nine lives as a cat."

"And with Val and me, you now have people to talk to, as well," I said.

"As a scholar and a warlock, I have no personal attachments whatsoever."

"You know, Barry, if I didn't know any better, I'd think you're actually growing fond of us," I said, laughing.

For the briefest of moments, the corners of Barry's mouth twitched.

"You'll never be able to prove it," he said.

***

We went up to Barry's library to prepare for the plan. I was itching to try out some new magic and now finally the chance had arisen. I was just about to get the wand out from its cardboard box when Barry stopped me in my tracks.

"You'll need your own wand, Amanda," he said. "I don't want you breaking mine. I'll need it soon myself, hopefully."

"But I don't have one," I said.

"Your great-aunt did," he said. "And that will work best

for you. Now, the only question is where it could be."

"I have no idea," I said. "it's not like the lawyer put it on the list of items. She'd have just thought it was some sort of stick."

"Yes, foolish indeed."

"May as well start looking here," I said, making for a small sideboard at the end of the room.

"Wait," Barry said, "it's not going to be in there."

"How do you know?"

"That's... that's where my things are in. Anyway, your great-aunt rarely used the library in her last years. She spent most of them in her room. The room you're sleeping in now, in fact."

We marched through the corridors until we had reached the bedroom. My things were already strewn throughout, giving it a pleasantly disordered look. Barry, who liked everything neat and tidy, raised an eyebrow.

"We will be lucky if we find anything at all in this mess," he said.

"Oh, stop moaning, Barry, I'm itching to try out some new spells," I said, eagerly looking around the room for any sign of the wand.

The search, hardly hampered by my own disorderliness I might point out, took the best part of half an hour. It turned out that my great-aunt had placed her most prized possessions in a little basket with a lid, which Barry had found at the top of the large cupboard.

Finally, I was holding the wand in my hand. It was made of black oak, with little ripples running all the way down the handle, making for a good, solid grip. A narrow band of white, smooth material – which I strongly suspected was ivory – snaked its way around the tip and the end of the handle.

"It's beautiful," I said.

"Yes, quite," Barry said. "Come on. We can't dawdle all day, we've got to interrogate Lady Worthington."

"You haven't even told me the plan yet."

Barry simply tapped his temple with his paw.

"All in here, Amanda. Now, we have to organise transport."

***

After checking in on Val one last time, I walked over to Mrs. Faversham's house to call Tom, the friendly taxi driver who had brought us here from the airport, to pick us up at Fickleton House. He didn't say anything about Barry at first, but when he saw him jump onto the backseat of the car, Tom suddenly became extremely agitated.

"Here, the cat's tearing into the seat. Get him off there," he said, uncharacteristically angry.

I lifted Barry up at once.

"I don't think there's any harm done. He's very well behaved. Keeps his claws in, but I'll keep him on my lap all the same."

Tom examined the seat. When he was satisfied that Barry had indeed not damaged the leather, he looked extremely relieved.

"Sorry for blowing my top. I – I just love this car. Replacements cost a fortune these days. So, where are you going, anyway?"

"Worthington Manor, please."

"You do seem to be visiting the high and mighty around here, don't you?" Tom said amicably.

Barry looked as if he was about to tell him just what he thought of the so-called high and mighty but I quickly thrust my hand in front of his mouth, pretending to stroke him. It wouldn't do for Tom to think he – or worse *we* – were crazy.

"Oh," I said. "we – I mean, I don't know her. It's just about the arts fair, that's all."

"Oh," Tom said, enthusiasm lighting up in his eyes.

"Are you coming to the fair, then? A good opportunity to get to know the locals. I'll introduce you to some, though God knows you wish I hadn't when I do."

He laughed again with his smoky wheeze.

"Are you an artist yourself?" I asked.

"Nah," he said. "Never really had the patience for it. But I enjoy a good painting here an' there. Especially, err, less modern ones, if you get my meaning."

***

A few minutes later, we had arrived at the driveway of Lady Worthington's large estate. Very unlike Fickleton House, which had a dilapidated charm about it, everything here ostentatiously screamed to any visitor that the inhabitants were rich as well as orderly.

Next to the immaculate hedges, large lion sculptures, painted gold, flanked the gates as we approached them. There was an intercom system on the right pillar with a fisheye camera above it. The metallic voice certainly didn't sound too welcoming as Tom manually rolled down the window to answer it.

At that moment, something sharp and painful penetrated the skin of my right hand.

"Ouch," I yelled. "What the…"

Barry was frantically jerking his head in the direction of the intercom and shaking his head, then pointing to me with his paw.

"I don't understand," I whispered, desperately trying not to be overheard by Tom, who was still wrestling with the window. "Shouldn't we say who we are?"

Barry nodded, relieved. Then, worried that I might misunderstand, shook his head furiously again. I patted him on the head, a gesture I knew he secretly enjoyed, and turned to Tom.

"It's alright, we'll get off here. I think… I think the cat

needs some exercise. We'll just walk up to the house," I said.

"You sure?" Tom said, slightly bewildered. "I can drop you off right in front of the house."

"No, no, that's quite alright. He's a little stressed. Too much tuna. We can enjoy the gardens along the way. Thanks again, Tom."

I paid him and got out of the taxi, away from the intercom and the camera. Still covered from view by the car, Barry and I swiftly moved behind the left pillar. I waved awkwardly to Tom as he backed out of the driveway and then turned to Barry, making sure we were well out of sight and earshot from the intercom and camera systems.

"Why didn't you tell me before you didn't want us recognised?" I demanded. "You don't have to go all Sherlock 'I'm going reveal everything at the end' Holmes on me, you know, Barry."

"I – I didn't think they'd have a camera," he said. "Don't look at me like that, Amanda. I'm a theoretician, not a prowler. I rarely have to think like a professional meddler, you know."

"Well, we're already meddling, so why don't you tell me the plan right now?"

"I think we need to alter your appearance a little bit," he said.

"Barry, I'm not transforming, if that's what you mean. I don't want to permanently turn into an old grandma or something. I'll be doing that naturally for long enough as it is."

"No, no," he hissed. "It's not a permanent charm – very different process. That's why we have to do it right before we enter. Nothing can go wrong."

"Famous last words…" I said rather facetiously but agreed to do it nonetheless.

"So what's the idea?" I asked. "Who do I turn into?"

"I think," Barry said slowly, "Lady Worthington will

only speak to someone she considers worth her time."

"Like the police?"

Barry shook his head irritably.

"That's strictly against magical law. Even if you're impersonating heb policemen, you'll get into serious trouble with the *Spellcasters' Association*. No, I think something else is in order. Something Lady Worthington is passionate about."

"So, an art expert or art dealer perhaps?" I said.

"Exactly," Barry said, rubbing his chin with his paw. "If you can make her believe you're a rich art patron, say, who is interested in her arts fair – interested in investing even – she'll definitely talk to you. We can move on from there."

"Pity we don't have Val with us," I said, wistfully. "Hope she's alright."

Barry clicked his tongue impatiently.

"Of course she is," he said. "Psychic fatigue, that's all. She'll be back on her feet tomorrow. Now, let's get on with it."

I nodded and got out my wand from my handbag. It felt very familiar by now, although I'd only held it a few times. Barry whispered the incantations to me and I performed them. It had been a lot more fun somehow to do magic without the pressure to succeed. Barry, though a seemingly endless source of magical knowledge, wasn't helping matters by being increasingly impatient.

Finally, he seemed satisfied, however. I took out the small mirror from my handbag and looked at my complexion. I got a shock at first, for my features were hardly recognisable. My nose and ears were a lot larger, and my entire face had aged by at least thirty years. My skin had lost most of its colour and was quite wrinkly.

"This isn't how I'm going to look in thirty years, is it?" I asked Barry.

"Worried?" Barry said smugly.

"If this is my future, perhaps I should be!"

"Keep your whiskers on, it's alright," he said. "These are generic short-term aging charms, mostly."

"So this isn't how I'm going to end up?" I asked.

"Nope," said Barry, with a sly grin. "Could be a lot worse."

"Very funny, Barry. Now, how do we proceed?"

Barry peaked his head suspiciously around the pillar, making sure nobody was there to overhear us.

"We gain entry under the pretence that you want to invest in the arts fair. Ask as many questions as possible, but don't be too transparent. If she smells a rat, we'll be kicked out by the butler before we can say 'arts fair'."

"How long do we have before the charms wear off?" I asked.

"About an hour," Barry said. "That's why we'd better move."

I nodded and led the way to the intercom system. I pressed the silver button below it and waited. After a little while, a pleasant female voice – very different from the one we had heard before in the car – answered.

"Worthington Manor, how can I help you?"

I cleared my throat.

"Hello, this is Mrs... erm... Merryweather. I'd like to talk to Lady Worthington about a contribution to her arts fair."

"Just a moment, please, Mrs. Merryweather. I'll tell Lady Worthington."

There was a clicking sound. Barry and I stood awkwardly in front of the gate, waiting.

"Merryweather?" he asked disbelievingly. "Honestly?"

"Oh, shut up, Barry," I said, taking the bait. "You come up with a good name next time, then. Wouldn't that be a job for our resident theoretician?"

"Evidently," he said drily.

Then, the intercom crackled again and the same female voice spoke.

"Lady Worthington will be with you shortly. Please come up the driveway."

"Thank you," I said.

The gates opened electronically. Barry, who wasn't used to any sort of technology since it didn't work at Fickleton House, was slightly unnerved. I noticed that he scampered rather quickly through gates, too.

"Harmless piece of technology, Barry," I said.

"Technology can go wrong," he said sulkily. "I'd trust magic any day."

"Like your transformation charms?" I asked.

"I think," he said, "your time would be better spent thinking about what to say to Lady Worthington rather than harassing and tormenting your magical mentor."

"Poor little you," I said with affection. "I'll think of something. And we have company, anyway."

A young, extremely thin woman in her early twenties was awaiting us in front of the main entrance to Worthington Manor. She was dressed in what I presumed to be an old-fashioned maid's uniform. It looked like something out of Downton Abbey.

If it was, however, it stood strangely at odds with the manor itself. I was by no means an expert in these things, of course, but the ostentatious display of wealth all around us, ranging from more golden statues similar to the lions at the gates to the silver handles on the water hoses, seemed to denigrate what must have once been a tasteful Georgian manor house. Even the curtains sparkled in the daylight from myriads of crystal glasses that had been woven into the material. Perhaps they were real diamonds. Or at least, that was the impression they were trying to make.

"Mrs. Merryweather?" the maid asked me, making a slight curtsey as she did so.

"Yes, that's right. I'm here to see Lady Worthington."

"Of course. Please excuse me, but the butler has fallen ill, quite unexpectedly. Upset tummy. So I've been answering the door. I'm Ethel, the maid, by the way. How do you do?"

"Nice to meet you, Ethel," I said.

"Please, follow me."

I nodded appreciatively. It was only at that moment that Ethel registered Barry's presence. Her eyes scanned his black fur and furrowed brow that gave him a permanently grumpy look.

"This is Barry, my cat. He goes everywhere I go. My companion, as it were. The only man in my life I can truly trust," I said, trying to pull off the crazy cat woman shtick. "I hope he can come in, too? I assure you, he is very well behaved and very clean."

"Oh, that's alright, then," she said. "Lady Worthington is usually quite strict about animals, but I'll see what I can do."

"Thank you," I said.

We entered through the main doors, which also sported golden knobs, and found ourselves in a long, high-ceiling hallway. Ethel was just about to march ahead when she seemed to remember something.

"Shall I take your coat, ma'am?" she asked.

"No, it's quite alright," I said, hanging it up on the stand myself.

Ethel looked rather relieved.

"Sorry, I'm just… not used to doing everything here at once. And I don't know when the butler will return."

"Nothing serious, I hope?" I asked.

Ethel hesitated, clearly pondering whether she should tell me or not. Finally, she had just made up her mind to do so when a sharp, ear-piercing call echoed through the house.

"ETHEL?"

"I'm sorry, that's Lady Worthington, I'll leave you in the library, if that's alright with you," she whispered.

Barry and I followed her through the hall. She beckoned

us to sit in one of the adjacent rooms, the library. The books, I noticed, were largely untouched, with a level of dust covering their jackets that I was sure wouldn't have been tolerated anywhere else in the house.

Meanwhile, we could hear Lady Worthington's booming voice from here.

"A cat?" she bellowed in disbelief.

Barry looked indignant. And for once, I quite agreed.

We couldn't hear Ethel's soft voice in response, but Lady Worthington had evidently been mollified by Ethel, at least for a while. A few moments later, Lady Worthington entered the library. She must have been in her late forties or early fifties, though her startlingly blonde hair, tied into an elegant bun, had no trace of grey at all. She was dressed in a morning robe which was just as ostentatious as the rest of her house. Her robe was black, with gold trimmings along the sides and cuffs. Her thick fingers sported an entire array of matching gold rings. Her manner was curt and unfriendly, her face sour and arrogant – no doubt an expression that had become permanent over the years.

"Yes?" she demanded, not even bothering to enter the room properly.

"Lady Worthington, my name is Merryweather. I hear that you are in charge of the upcoming arts fair in Fickleton?"

"That is correct," she said, eyeing Barry with dislike. "We won't be taking any more artistic contributions, however. If that's what you're after."

"No, quite the contrary," I said. "I deal in exquisite pieces of art, you see, and I'm always on the lookout for a good investment."

Immediately, I saw that I had struck conversational gold. At the sound of money, her every particle lit up. I had her full attention now. Her manner changed as if someone had pulled a switch. She flashed her artificially whitened teeth at me.

"Please forgive me, Mrs... Merryweather, did you say? And what a beautiful cat you have. I do so adore them. Yes, you've certainly come to the right place. We have an impressive assortment of backers already, but I'm sure we'll find a spot for just one more. Well, why don't you join me in the morning room? I rarely use this place here, too many stuffy books."

She laughed and beckoned me to follow her. Barry and I complied, though we couldn't refrain from exchanging looks with raised eyebrows once she had turned her back to us. Even Barry, a natural cynic in regard to both warlocks and humans, was taken aback by Lady Worthington.

Outside in the corridor, Lady Worthington snapped her fingers at Ethel.

"Tea for three," she ordered.

Ethel inclined her head in deference and bustled off down the hallway.

"Please, in here. So much more light from outside in the morning room. My husband always joins me here in the afternoon. He likes to work deep into the night. So we should have some peace until he comes downstairs. *Men*."

I forced myself to laugh along with her. Privately, of course, I certainly couldn't blame him. He probably had all the reason to avoid her as much as possible.

Lady Worthington had been right about the morning room, however. Though the cherubs on the mantelpiece were quite tacky, the rest of the room was in much better taste than the other rooms I had been able to peek into along the way here. She sat down on a comfortable-looking armchair and beckoned me towards the adjacent sofa.

"I think, Mrs. Merryweather, you will find that we have many talented artists among us. All producing cutting-edge art for the 21st century. An excellent investment, to be sure."

"I have no doubt," I said. "There are a few things I'd like to clear up before I can commit myself, however. I hope you understand, Lady Worthington."

"Oh, I understand perfectly," she said, flashing her toothy smile again. "A very wise decision. What would you like to know?"

"Well, it has more to do with the... village affairs than anything else, I suppose," I said. "There have been rumours of a death – a murder even – in the local pub over in Fickleton."

"A murder..." Lady Worthington repeated blankly.

"Yes, a journalist, I believe."

Her expression was unreadable as her gaze fixed itself on me. I could tell she was doing some hard thinking all the while. I kept her gaze, trying to appear as innocent and as non-judgmental as possible.

"Nosworthy," Lady Worthington breathed, her nostrils flaring. "Yes, I've heard of her."

"So she wasn't too popular, then?"

Lady Worthington scoffed at the question. At that moment, Ethel appeared in the doorway with a tray. She walked over to us and set it down on the table, quietly handing us our teas. I thanked Ethel, though Lady Worthington didn't even acknowledge her presence. Instead, she continued our conversation.

"Of course not. A nosy busybody if ever I saw one. Journalist my hat. Trying to cook up trouble wherever she went, that's what she was. And then, of course, she got herself killed."

"But nobody knows who did it?" I asked, trying to contain my eagerness.

Lady Worthington gave me another of her hard looks. Ethel, who looked even more nervous than ever, fumbled with the sugar and accidently spilt it all over the carpet.

"Oh, you silly girl!" Lady Worthington exclaimed. "Clean this up, go on. What do I pay you for? And bring us another bowl of sugar."

Ethel, struck numb from shock, dropped to her knees

62

and began sweeping up the sugar with her hands. I was just about to help her when I felt the sting of Barry's claws on my ankle. He was ever so slightly mouthing the word 'no', facing away from Lady Worthington as best he could. He was right, of course. As much as I felt sorry for Ethel, I couldn't show too much concern if I wanted any more information from Lady Worthington.

"Excuse my clumsy maid, Mrs. Merryweather, you were saying?"

"Erm… yes, so the perpetrator hasn't been apprehended yet?"

"No," she said. "Not that I know of, at least. And I don't really care if they catch him, to be perfectly frank with you. It may sound harsh, Mrs. Merryweather, but the deceased woman was not a very nice person. She made a great deal of trouble for many of the inhabitants, both in Fickleton and the surrounding villages. That poor young man – Derek Reynolds – for example."

"Derek Reynolds?"

There was a name I hadn't heard before. Ethel left the room again with the empty tray and the mopped-up sugar, still shaking slightly. Then, I felt the most strange tingling sensation in my face and my hands. Horrified, I looked at Barry, indicating my hands. He made a whirling sign with his paw that clearly said that I had to accelerate the conversation somehow. The effects of my spells were beginning to wear off.

"Yes," Lady Worthington said, sipping her tea and luckily paying no attention to us, "Mr. Reynolds runs the local golf club. An honest businessman, who naturally attracts a lot of envy from the locals and the press. Quite like myself, of course."

"And did the deceased journalist give you any trouble in regard to the arts fair?" I asked.

She mustered me again. I was pushing it now. I could tell that only the prospect of a juicy cheque kept her from kicking me out.

"You've heard of my little encounter with her, I take it?" she said.

"Well, yes, it did come up at some point. I just wanted to make sure that, erm, any investment I make is free from scandal," I said apologetically, as Ethel re-entered with a fresh bowl of sugar.

Lady Worthington's nostrils widened again.

"I would not pay too much attention to village gossip if I were you," she said. "And I don't like your insinuations. Yes, I had a quarrel with the murdered journalist, but so did everyone else who had the misfortune of coming across her. Mr. Reynolds, myself. Even Colonel Warton. Now that's a shady character whenever I saw one. Perhaps she had a closer look at that illegal gun collection of his. Or the ivory he's had smuggled over here. *And* he prowls the streets at night like some criminal for God knows what reason."

She leaned closer to me, setting her tea aside.

"Now, I wasn't even out at the time she died," Lady Worthington continued. "I was here, at Worthington Manor. With my beloved husband. Not that it's any of your business, of course. But one must crush these malicious rumours where one can."

She stared at me, a determined expression on her face. Ethel, who had been listening to every word, rooted to the spot, suddenly dropped the second, fresh bowl of sugar, which once more landed on the carpet. Lady Worthington shrieked in anger.

"There, see what you have done. You are upsetting my staff, Mrs. Merryweather. I must insist that you leave at once."

There was nothing else I could do. I got up, with Barry following in my wake. Once more, Ethel was crouched on the carpet, frantically brushing the sugar into her cupped apron. Lady Worthington was towering over her, making her best effort to ignore me as I made for the door.

I stepped out into the hallway, taking a deep breath as I did so. I could hear Lady Worthington berating poor Ethel in the morning room. Barry and I slowly walked along the corridor until we couldn't hear Lady Worthington's dulcet tones any longer.

"Quite the dragon," I whispered to him.

He simply nodded in agreement, still fearful of being overheard by another member of the staff.

In the hall, I was just about to get my coat when, to my surprise, Ethel hurried down the corridor towards us.

"Mrs. Merryweather?" she asked, nervously checking whether Lady Worthington had followed her. "Do you have a moment?"

"Of course," I said.

"It's just… Lady Worthington, well, she didn't quite tell you the truth."

"What do you mean?" I asked.

"She wasn't here on the night when that journalist was killed. I know because I was here all the time, doing extra hours and…"

But at that moment, Lady Worthington's robed figure entered into the hallway. Her eyes narrowed further at the sight of Ethel talking to me.

"Out of my house, at once," she said dangerously. "Ethel, I forbid you to talk to this woman. Good day."

Ethel gave me a desperate look.

"She can talk to whomever she likes," I said as I opened the front door. "She is not your slave, Lady Worthington – whatever you might think. Good day."

I left her fuming at the door. I could sense she wanted to give a retort but couldn't think of anything in time. So, with the satisfaction of having the last word, Barry and I walked down the driveway towards the gates through which we had entered. From afar, I could still hear her rage and shout at Ethel.

"She's even more horrible than you'd made her out to be," I said to Barry once we were safely out of earshot.

"Yes," he said. "A nasty piece of work. But what can you expect from new money?"

"Hey, I'm new money as well," I said, mocking indignation.

"Well," he said. "At least you don't act like it. And you inherited."

"Thanks, Barry. I guess. Anyway, d'you think Ethel will be alright? I mean, she was almost raving mad in there."

Barry frowned. I could tell that the encounter had disturbed him, too. Finally, he nodded his feline head heavily.

"She's spiteful enough, but I don't think she's stupid. I doubt she'll harm her, at least physically, that is. Though for her psychological well-being, another employer would certainly be in order."

"Yes," I said. "Especially if she turns out to be our killer in the end."

CHAPTER 7

Back at Fickleton House, we quickly told Val all about our encounter during dinner. She was still looking a little pale but much better than when we had left her. She was evidently adapting well to her new powers. Her appetite had also returned.

"So, d'you think it was Lady Worthington, Amy?" Val asked, cutting up her fish.

"I don't know. I wouldn't put it past her."

"That poor maid. Ethel, you said her name was? Is there anything we can do?"

Barry shook his head. We had finally given in to his demands of sitting at the table with us. He was perched on top of a tower of cushions piled on one of the chairs so that he could reach his plate on the table.

"It's a free country," said Barry. "She's free to find another employer whenever she chooses to."

"Yes but that's not always an option. I could have killed my boss a couple of times, too. But getting a new job isn't a laughing matter. You know how it is."

He looked at me with a blank expression.

"Or perhaps you don't," I said, winking at Val.

"Yeah, Barry, do warlocks have jobs?" Val asked.

"Some do, certainly. I, however, had a *mission*. Still have, as a matter of fact. Very different," he said.

"So what's the next step, anyway?" Val said, trying to avert a lecture on theoretical magic as quickly as possible.

"I think we should question more people. This Reynolds man she mentioned. He runs a golf club. And Colonel…"

"Colonel Warton," Barry said. "Yes, he's a well-known figure around here. Strange fellow, mind you. Perhaps we should start with the Colonel."

"Yes," Val said excitedly. "But this time, I'll be coming with you."

***

The next day, after another one of Mrs. Faversham's hearty breakfasts, we walked down into the village to visit Colonel Warton. With only a few days before Lady Worthington's arts fair and a mere week left before Christmas, most villagers we passed were in an excellent mood. It was also a good opportunity to get to know some of them, as they tended to their cars or decorated their gardens for Christmas, much to Barry's distaste for social interaction.

Colonel Warton's house was located at the very edge of the village. Whatever the festive mood of the other inhabitants, Colonel Warton's house certainly didn't reflect it. Unlike the cosy little English houses surrounding it, it was made of pure concrete with a corrugated iron roof. A large fence surrounded it on all sides, making it resemble some sort of high-security facility. It wouldn't have been out of place in a film on the Soviet Union.

We approached the heavy front door, which looked like the fireproof doors you'd often find in the cellars of houses. There was no intercom system, but a spyhole next to the door told us that we wouldn't be able to enter without prior scrutiny.

I extended my hand and rang the bell. We waited for a while, but there was no answer.

"Maybe he's out?" Val said.

"If he is," Barry said softly. "It's almost unheard of. Legend has it that he only leaves the house after dark. Hates the villagers, you see. Can't say I blame him particularly on that front, though not for the same reasons, naturally."

"Oh, Barry, you *are* insufferable," Val said affectionately.

I pushed the doorbell again.

"Well, Barry, you have a point with PC Bowler," I said "But surely they aren't all like that…"

"Wait a minute, I think I saw something in the garden, beyond the fence. Over there," Val said.

Val was right. A figure dressed in grey was slouching around the garden with a shovel in his hand. This, I was sure, had to be Colonel Warton. We approached the fence. Immediately, a pair of dogs – unseen to us – started barking furiously.

"Any last minute transformations, Barry?" I said, trying to make myself heard over the noise from the dogs.

"No, I don't think so this time," he said. "We might stand a better chance if he knows we're from here."

Val called out to the Colonel. Perhaps it was a little too friendly for his liking, for he eyed us suspiciously from afar for a while before limping over to us. He took out some sort of remote control from his pocket and pressed a button. A metallic clunking was followed by rapid canine footsteps. Two of the largest German shepherd dogs I had ever seen in my life scampered to their master's side, still barking at what all three of them considered to be an intrusion. Certainly, I was glad to have a fence between me and those dogs. Barry, however, seemed paralysed by fear. He was shaking silently beside us. I didn't blame him. Warlock or not, the dogs were about five times his size. They'd rip him – and probably Val and me too – to shreds in a matter of seconds.

I was startled at Colonel Warton's appearance when he approached the fence and we could get a closer look at him. His eyes were bloodshot, and his nose was extremely red, with burst blood vessels all over his crinkly face. His hair was kept short in a military style, though his crumpled grey coat would never have passed inspection.

He reached down to his dogs with two gnarled hands. They stopped barking at once. It was evident that Colonel Warton had absolute authority over them. They licked his hands, more as an act of submission than affection, and then remained perfectly still, their eyes following our every move.

"Excuse me, are you Colonel Warton?" I asked.

"That's right," he said hoarsely. "Who's asking?"

"My name is Amanda. This is Val and this is B-"

I was just about to introduce Barry but quickly stopped myself in my tracks. I kept forgetting that, to everyone else, Barry was simply a cat. And that was the way it had to be.

"What do you want?" he said.

"We just moved here, you see. To Fickleton House. Do you know it?" I said.

"Everybody knows Fickleton House around here," he said.

"Yes, well. We just wanted to get to know everyone in the village. Introduce ourselves."

"That's right," Val said, trying to contribute. "We've heard a lot about you."

Turning to Val, Colonel Warton emitted something between a harsh laugh and a cough.

"Oh, you have, have you? All lies. Don't believe a word they say. They never liked me around here. And I don't mind. I don't like them, either."

"Erm, yes, why don't we sit down together? Have a little chat."

"We're having a chat right now," he said stubbornly. "And I like it out here. The cold winter air keeps me sharp. And the dogs aren't allowed in the house, anyway. I like to keep them around. Keep me protected."

"Protected? From whom?" I asked.

"The villagers, of course."

"Have they... threatened you?" Val said.

"There are signs," he said mysteriously. "They don't care for ex-army much. Probably reminds them they didn't do anything for their country. All they ever do is talk about diets and green lifestyle and all that rubbish. Never seen the real world. Never had to fight for anything except their flat-screen TVs."

"But something did happen here a few nights ago… a journalist was murdered in the pub," I said.

Colonel Warton scoffed.

"Oh, her, yes. A nosy parker if ever I saw one. But like all meddlers, didn't know when to stop. Yes, they did her in alright. Didn't surprise me in the least when I heard the news."

"Do… do you know who did it?" I asked.

"Of course not. I would have reported it to PC Bowler. Only right thing to do. Pity he doesn't have any brains, though. He couldn't catch a murderer if he was living next to the police station."

Val and I couldn't quite suppress our nervous laughter.

"What?" he said, immediately suspicious again. "What did I say?"

"Oh, nothing," I said. "It's just that PC Bowler accused me the other day. And I wasn't even in the area when the murder occurred."

"Fits the picture, alright," he said, nodding his head. "If they can pin it on someone, they will. I'd mind my step if I were you. Lady Worthington and that Reynolds boy have the entire community in their pockets. Funded a new community centre, even. Nobody dares point the finger. But we all know…"

"Do you think Michelle Nosworthy – the journalist – was investigating them?"

"Yes, that's what I reckon," Colonel Warton said. "I would have helped that young woman if she hadn't been so blooming curious about my… well, never mind. Makes me suspicious, anyhow. If you ask me, there's definitely something dodgy going on. And it's got to do with that arts fair."

"We heard that the journalist's notebook was stolen. Do you know anything about that?"

"No, I don't," he said.

At that moment, one of the large German shepherds started growling, keenly observing Barry, who was still frozen to the spot in terror.

"Time to feed the dogs," Colonel Warton said suddenly. "Don't want them to eat the cat, now, do we?"

He gave off a short laugh that sounded more like a bark.

"Quite," I said, forcing myself to smile. "Well, thank you, Colonel. That was very… informative."

He narrowed his eyes.

"Let me give you some advice. Stay out of this. It's not worth it. And they're too powerful. They've killed before. And they'll kill again. You mark my words."

***

Back on the main road of the village, Val turned to me excitedly.

"Amy, he's hiding something. Colonel Warton, I mean. I – I felt it when you were talking to him."

"Well he did admit that the killed journalist was poking around his place, asking questions. Do you think it was that?"

"No, it's not that," Val said. "It was when you mentioned the notebook. He was definitely withholding information."

"Do you think he could be our murderer?" I asked.

"I don't know," said Val. "But he knows something about the notebook. I'm sure of it."

"He might have stolen it," said Barry, who was trotting alongside us. "That's what I would do. Get rid of the evidence. Perhaps she had something on his collection."

"Yes," I said, frowning. "He'd certainly try to destroy it as quickly as possible if she could have proven that it was illegally obtained. What do you think, Val?"

"I'm sorry, Amy. It's all just so… so *vague*. All I know is that he felt a keen sting of fear when you mentioned the notebook. And relief when he was able to change the subject."

"So he could be our murderer," I said.

"But he warned you against the villagers himself," said Val.

"Precisely," said Barry darkly. "It might have been a veiled warning. A warning to stay out of his way."

***

We decided to see Mr. Reynolds next, the young golf club owner. It wasn't hard to find out where the club was from the local bakery, as the girl behind the counter was very talkative. The club was only two miles outside of the village, and it appeared that Reynolds himself had funded a pedestrian pathway that led directly to his club.

After a quick stop at the bank (I still had to get used to the fact that my balance wasn't in a perpetual state of negative figures), Barry was all for calling Tom to drive us there, but Val and I insisted on walking.

"The exercise will do you some good, Barry," Val said.

Barry was grumpily trotting behind us.

"This body was built for a couple of years' use only," he said. "Not for decades of plodding around the countryside with a clumsy psychic and a novice witch."

But even Barry couldn't deny that it had been a good idea. A gentle cover of snow had fallen during the night, covering the beautiful meadows around us in a coat of white. The pathway itself was firm and far enough from the main road to ensure an enjoyable walk to the club, free of the noise of cars and busses. It was country life at its best, and all of us thoroughly enjoyed it.

Finally, we reached the golf club. I was surprised by the amount of activity there. I'd never played golf myself, but I had somehow assumed it would be closed in this weather.

Yet the area next to the busy car park – probably for beginners – was packed with guests and instructors in heavy winter wear and gloves, practicing on the green that had been cleared of snow.

Next to it stood the club itself, an impressive array of buildings, especially for such a small community. We walked into the main entrance of the 'Fickleton Golf Club' and found ourselves in a reception area. A large screen announced the various activities on offer. There was a lot more than golf. It appeared that the club had its own hotel, a swimming pool, a gym, a restaurant, and several conference rooms for business purposes. Squash and various other sports activities were also on offer. Reynolds, by all accounts, was doing well. I approached the reception desk.

"Excuse me, I'd like to talk to Mr. Reynolds," I said.

A smartly dressed woman in her thirties smiled apologetically behind the desk.

"I'm afraid he isn't available at the moment. Is there anything I can do?"

"Do you know when he will be back?" I asked.

"I'm sorry, I don't. I can tell him you called. Shall I leave a message?"

"No, thank you."

I went over to where Barry and Val were waiting. Many people, families mostly, had arrived with their pets, so nobody seemed to be bothered by Barry. Val was carrying him in her arms, just in case.

"She won't say where he is," I said, annoyed. "Looks like we've hit a dead end."

"Aren't we forgetting something?" Barry whispered in my ear, balancing on Val's arms to get closer to me.

"What do you mean?"

"You're a witch for crying out loud," he hissed. "Use magic."

"Oh, yes, of course. I've got my wand in my handbag

here somewhere. What spell can I use on her, do you think?"

"A simple agreeableness charm ought to do the trick," said Barry. "If she really doesn't know where he is, we'll have to try something else."

He whispered the instructions and the precise incantation into my ear.

"OK, got it. Thanks, Barry."

Casting the spell without being seen was quite another matter, however. I pretended to be interested in the potted plants at the side of the desk, above which hung the various framed prizes the club had won since it had been established. Thankfully, the receptionist didn't appear to be particularly interested in anything but her smartphone, which was tucked in tightly at the very corner of the desk. I snuck my wand out of my bag and slipped it past the desk on the far side, away from the entrance area.

"Gratus," I murmured under my breath.

Light sparks emitted from the end of my wand, hitting the receptionist's leg. A terrible shot. I hoped that it would be enough, but it was hard to aim properly at such an angle. I decided to try my luck.

"Excuse me, could I speak to Mr. Reynolds, please? I think he'd want to talk to me, too."

"Of course, I'm sure he will make an exception," the receptionist said with a rather vague smile on her face. "He should be in the squash room. It's two floors down from here. You can take the elevator to your right."

***

A few minutes later, we found ourselves in a very long corridor of the gym area. The rooms leading off it were full of sweating brows and red faces, all furiously engaged in one activity or another. From what I could tell from the open doors and signs I was able to read in time as we passed by, there were rooms for table tennis, bowling, boxing, gymnastics and dancing, as well as a small football area for kids. At last, we reached the squash area.

The walls were see-through. A man and a woman were inside, playing an energetic match. They were both wearing sport outfits all in white. If this had been the 1980s, I thought to myself, the only thing missing would have been the headbands. Undoubtedly, the man was handsome and possessed a certain flair, his tanned skin and blond hair clashing spectacularly with his white clothes. The blonde woman at his side, only a couple of years younger than I was perhaps, was exceptionally good-looking.

"Excuse me," a man said. "Would you mind? You're blocking the way."

"Oh, sorry, by all means," I said, as we moved forward.

We had all been strangely entranced by the couple in the glass cage in front of us. At that moment, Barry gave a low whistle in appreciation of the blonde woman inside the squash room. The man who had passed turned around and, seeing only two women and a cat, flashed a grin at me and made a rather forthright gesture. I hastily shook my head, waving my hands to show him it was a misunderstanding. He looked rather disappointed but went on his way all the same.

"Barry!" I hissed.

"What?" he said.

"Stop whistling when there're men passing. They'll think Val or I whistled," I said.

"Yeah, we want to whistle when we want to," said Val.

"I was simply expressing my approval of the young lady playing squash, that's all," said Barry. "I don't get out that much."

"Well, now we know why," I said.

"I didn't know cats could whistle," Val said.

"I had a lot of time to practice," Barry said defensively. "You'd be surprised what you can…"

"Shush, you two," I whispered. "Look, they're having a quarrel by the looks of it."

It was true. The woman had thrown her racket to the floor and was pointing her finger angrily at the man, who was making swiping movements, as if to dismiss what she was saying. The glass was evidently sound-proof as we watched them rage at each other in silence for a little while until Val said:

"I think they're coming out. Careful."

All three of us quickly pretended to be reading the gym schedule on the wall.

"Not you, Barry," I hissed. "Cats can't read, remember?"

"Oh, yes, sorry," he said. "Didn't bring my spectacles anyway."

The glass door to the squash room swung open and the blonde woman rushed outside.

"Wait," the man called after her.

But it was too late. She had already slammed the door in his face and stormed down the corridor. Apparently, he was considering whether he should follow her, but, seeing so many guests around, thought better of it. I decided to quickly take advantage of the situation.

"Are you Mr. Reynolds?" I asked.

"That's me," he said, his gaze lingering on Barry for a moment.

"Nice to meet you. I'm Amanda Sheridan. I just moved into Fickleton House the other day."

It was remarkable how fast a face could change from bored indifference to opportunistic enthusiasm.

"Ah, yes, nice to meet you indeed. We were all wondering who'd be inheriting the estate. I know Mrs. Sharpe, you know, does a lot of work for the club as well. Old friend. Knew the old lady, too, in fact. Was she your grandmother?"

"My great-aunt. But I'd never met her."

"It must have been quite a surprise to you, then," he said. "If you need any help with the estate, I can connect you with a few of my people. I understand running such a place can be quite costly, even though that's hardly a problem now, eh?"

He laughed heartily.

"That would be wonderful," I said, feigning interest. "But right now, Val and I are trying to figure out whether we want to stay here, in the Cotswolds."

Val looked at me in bewilderment.

"But…" she began.

"Aren't we, Val?" I said, emphasising every syllable.

"Oh, yes, that's right. We are. Still wondering."

"Well, anything I can do to help make up your mind?" he said, flashing a smile at both of us. Either the quarrel with his lady friend was forgotten or he was an excellent actor.

"There is, in fact. We're rather concerned with… erm… the security in this area. I heard there was a death in the pub in Fickleton the other day. There's even talk of murder. We just wouldn't want to move into an area that's… you know."

Reynolds dropped his smile immediately.

"Yes, ghastly business," he said. "I understand that you're concerned. However, if you want my opinion, you aren't in any danger. I mean, it's not like you're walking around the village and asking a lot of silly questions like that journalist."

Val and I gulped.

"Do you know what happened to her?" Val asked.

Reynolds shook his handsome head.

"No," he said. "I was having dinner at the time at an excellent Italian place with my girlfriend. You might have seen her. I was playing squash with her until a few minutes ago. Anyway, I took a taxi home and that's that. Didn't even hear about it until the following day from one of my employees. Now, you'll have to excuse me. My girlfriend is rather cross with me. I'll just have to see whether she is alright. Nice to meet you both."

He shook my hand and then Val's. His gaze lingered once more on Barry before briskly walking down the corridor.

"What do you make of him, Val?" I asked her when he was safely out of sight. The corridor was empty apart from us now.

"Difficult to say. I don't think he was telling the entire truth just then. When he was talking about the night of the murder. But the vibes are very faint with him."

"Might be a sign of a sorcerer, mightn't it?" I said excitedly, turning to Barry.

"It might," Barry said softly. "In fact, a trained sorcerer will almost certainly be able to dampen Val's abilities. There are some hebs who can do it, too, however. Naturals, you might call them. Not uncommon at all in shrewd business men like Reynolds."

"So there's no way to tell?" Val asked him, her face drooping slightly in disappointment.

"There are psychics who can. It takes many years of practice." said Barry.

"Well, we don't have years. So what should we do?" Val asked.

"I think I want to find out more about Mr. Reynolds and his girlfriend," I said. "I won't be a minute."

"Wait, Amy. Where are you going?"

"Later, Val. It'll be too suspicious if all three of us go darting all over the place. Wait for me in the restaurant. I'll be right up. I just want to check something."

There was no time to explain. I tore down the corridor in the direction that Reynolds had disappeared. If my hunch was right, they were continuing their quarrel elsewhere, provided Reynolds had found her, that is.

The door at the end of the corridor led to yet another one. How big could a place get, I thought to myself. But I continued down them, passing tennis courts, young men lifting weights, old men in swimming pools and in the sauna with towels wrapped around them, until I reached a dead end. This was evidently the end of the gym area, marked by a staff bathroom and a caretaker's broom cupboard.

I was just about to turn back when I heard a familiar male voice.

"Keep your voice down, for Heaven's sake."

Yes, that was undoubtedly Reynolds. And it was coming from the staff bathroom just a few feet away. The voices were very faint, too faint to hear anything. I had to get closer somehow. Very gently, I opened the door to the bathroom. But the clicking noise of the door must have alerted them, because they fell silent immediately. I hastily let the door fall in place again.

Panicking slightly, I grabbed at the handle of the broom cupboard next to it. It was open. I quickly slipped inside and closed the door behind me. It was pitch black in here and I fumbled blindly for the light but couldn't find it. The wall to the bathroom, I noticed with delight, must have been a lot thinner from this side. I was able to make out almost every word they were saying.

"Who was it?" asked a woman's voice.

"Nobody, probably just a lost customer or something," Reynolds said.

His voice was a lot harsher and deeper than when he had spoken to me a few minutes earlier. He was in an aggressive mood.

"It's too risky, Derek," his girlfriend said. "What if someone finds out? I don't want to be part of this."

"You already are, Patricia. If you want to continue going out with me, you'd better do what I say," Reynolds said.

"And if you want to go out with *me*, Derek, you'd better tell me the whole story with that awful journalist woman."

"Calm down, the customers will hear us," Reynolds said.

"I don't care, Derek," Patricia said. "Let them hear how

you cheated on me behind my back, how you lied to me for weeks. And… and now, you're lying to the police, too."

"I'm not lying," he spluttered.

"Yes, you are, Derek. I've tolerated all your little… quirks and that stuff but… this is withholding evidence."

"I can't tell them about the affair. They're just dying to find someone with a motive. They'll bang me up before you can say 'unfair'. Is that what you want? See me arrested by that buffoon PC Bowler? The police are just looking for a scapegoat for this case. I'm just preventing them from wasting their time with an innocent man, that's all. You know I'm innocent, don't you?"

"I… well, yes… of course. Derek, I…"

"Then keep your mouth shut and don't talk to anyone about this," Reynolds said. "Because if they ever find out I didn't take the taxi here that night but got off at the pub to… to see her, I'm toast."

CHAPTER 8

Still hiding in the broom cupboard, I stood perfectly still, waiting for the conversation between Derek Reynolds and his girlfriend Patricia to continue. Either they had lowered their voices again or weren't talking at all, however. I had an impending sense that I had overstayed my welcome. I had heard enough to get going with in any event.

I fumbled for the door knob and turned it as quietly as I could, peaking through the crack as I did so. The coast seemed to be clear. I stepped out and was just about to close the door when my handbag, which had somehow got caught on something inside the broom cupboard, fell from my shoulder and crashed into some dustbins below.

"Did you hear that?" I heard Reynolds exclaim from the caretaker's bathroom.

There was no time to be lost. Frantically, I yanked at my handbag as hard as I could and tore down the corridor, trying to gain as much space between Reynolds and myself before he opened the door. I heard him yank it open behind me.

"Hey, you, wait a minute," he said.

I turned around in mock surprise. He eyed me with suspicion as his girlfriend peeked around the corner behind him to get a look.

"Oh, fancy seeing you here, Mr. Reynolds," I said.

"Yes, quite. May I ask what you are looking for?" he said, trying to remain as calm and collected as possible. "Perhaps I can help you find your way."

"Oh, I was just looking at the various activities you have on offer down here. Like…"

I spun around desperately, reading the only sign that I could read from where I was standing.

"… water aerobics for the elderly."

"Water aerobics for the elderly?" he asked in disbelief.

"Erm, yes," I said. "Old age may hit you before you know it, that's what my mother always used to say."

That was terrible. Where was Val to shut me up when I needed her? Reynolds looked at me with narrowed eyes. I could see his temper rising beneath that friendly mask he wore for customers.

"Well, I'd better be off," I said awkwardly. "Goodbye."

"Goodbye, Miss Sheridan," Reynolds said. "And do let me know how water aerobics worked out for you."

***

Upstairs, I found Val and Barry at the back of the restaurant. I quickly filled them in on what had happened. Barry didn't appear particularly surprised, though Val was incensed.

"How could he? That's the lowest of the low, cheating on her like that. Absolutely disgusting. She shouldn't put up with something like that."

"Val," I said patiently. "We aren't the vice squad. We're here to get *me* off the hook, remember? Before that moronic PC Bowler can frame me."

"Yes," Barry said, buried in thought. "But perhaps Reynolds is guilty of both cheating on his girlfriend and murder. After all, a love gone sour or the wish to cover up an affair might easily lead to murder."

"So might jealousy," I said. "Think of the girlfriend. Perhaps she followed Reynolds that night when he visited the journalist and killed her afterwards."

"She should have done *him* in, instead," Val said, then adding after seeing our raised eyebrows: "Oh, come on, you know what I mean. I just don't like people cheating on each other."

"And a good sentiment it is, Valerie," Barry said. "One

that the modern world doesn't care for, of course."

"So, another suspect on the list, then?" Val said quickly before Barry could tell us yet again how much better life was in the 1950s when he was a young man.

"It seems so," I said. "The more people we question, the longer the list gets. And apparently, everyone had a motive for killing the journalist. Lady Worthington's art fair and her dodgy alibi that was put in doubt by Ethel. Colonel Warton and his illegal collection of weapons and whatever else he's got hidden in his bunker of a house. And now Reynolds and his affair with the victim. Whatever next?"

***

We decided to eat an early dinner at the restaurant and walk back to Fickleton House. When we finally set foot on the pathway back to the village, it was already getting dark. Usually, I didn't mind the dark particularly, but I had to admit that I felt slightly uncomfortable doing so now. All the talk about murderers and victims had got to me. Val, apparently, felt quite the same way.

"We should have called Tom to drive us back," she said.

"Yeah," I agreed. "Too late now, though. We're close to the woods. We'll definitely do that next time, though."

"I don't mind in the slightest. My eyesight is excellent in the dark," Barry said. "So no need to worry. I will guide you."

"A great help you'll be if the murderer pounces on us," Val said.

"He won't pounce, he'll most likely cast a curse," said Barry. "Anyway, we're almost there. We can take the shortcut up here, leads directly to the entrance of the gardens at the back of the house."

We followed Barry into the woods. Where the soft cover of snow had provided a little reflective light along the way from the golf club, it was almost entirely dark here. We were barely able to see Barry a few feet in front of us, but no more.

"Arghh."

Val had suddenly disappeared.

"Val, where are you?"

"Down here, I must have tripped."

I helped her up to her feet again, brushing snow and old leaves from her coat.

"Sorry," she said. "Bit creepy in the woods."

"Don't worry," I said. "I guess it's getting to all of us. Nobody's here, Val. It's OK."

We were just about to set off again when a bright light from a torch was flung in our faces, blinding us.

"Who goes there?" a surly voice addressed us from afar.

It was Colonel Warton. And he wasn't alone, either. The soft but audible growling told me that he had brought one of his enormous German shepherd dogs with him. Barry had clearly come to the same conclusion and skidded towards us, seeking refuge behind Val and me. I started fidgeting for my wand in my handbag, just in case.

"Colonel," I said. "What... what a surprise. Fancy meeting you in the woods around here. Isn't your house at the other end of the village?"

"I like to take long walks," he said. "And Rex here needs some exercise."

"Quite. Well, we'll be on our way then," I said.

"Not so fast," he said menacingly.

He lowered his torch so that we could see him properly for the first time. He looked as worn-out as ever, though there was an odd glint in his eye that hadn't been there earlier. He reached down to the massive hound at his side and caressed it behind its ears, which stood up in a state of constant vigilance. I could sense Barry quivering behind me. And to be honest, as I looked at those large fangs of the German shepherd, I couldn't blame him. I was feeling sick myself.

"They say these woods are haunted," Colonel Warton continued, slowly shuffling towards us, his hound close at his heels. "That's why I like coming here. Less chance of meeting the natives. You remember what I told you?"

"Which bit exactly?" I asked, gripping my wand a little tighter.

"About keeping out of this business," he said.

"Vividly," I said.

"It's dangerous," he said. "The villagers – you can't trust them. Don't be fooled by their fancy houses and cars. They're rotten to the core, the lot of them. And they're out to get me. I know it. I think I'll let the dogs sleep in the house tonight. Yes, they won't dare come in then. You keep out of trouble, now."

"We will," I said, trying to get the conversation over with as fast as possible. "You… you be safe, too, Colonel."

He stared at me as if nobody had ever said something like that to him in his entire life. Then, he nodded brusquely.

"You're alright."

He slowly shuffled past us, with Rex, his monster of a dog, following him in perfect obedience. The dog's eyes, however, were fixated on Barry until his canine neck wouldn't allow it to turn any further.

"He's crazy," said Val once she could be sure that we wouldn't be overheard. "Totally paranoid."

"Yes," I said. "Come on, let's get back to the house."

But Barry wouldn't move. He stood there, frozen.

"Barry," Val said, lifting him up from the ground. "Barry, are you alright?"

Being hoisted up must have awoken him again.

"It's… nothing," he said faintly. "I just… just can't stand German shepherds."

With Val carrying Barry, we pressed on for another few minutes through the woods until finally we could see the moon properly again. It was remarkable what power of illumination it had once the clouds had retreated sufficiently and we were out in the open again.

As Barry had promised, we found ourselves at the back of Fickleton House. We entered the gardens through a small wooden gate. We were close to Mrs. Faversham's house, which stood only a few feet away. A light burning in the front room told us that she was still up and about. We walked through the garden and reached the back door of Fickleton House. Cold but glad to be home, I unlocked it and let us in.

I was tired but there was no way I was going to sleep anytime soon after our walk through the woods and the eerie chat with Colonel Warton, so I decided to start a fire in one of the sitting rooms on the ground floor I hadn't used before. It was small and comfortable, facing the front yard and garden.

Val, who insisted on trying out some new cocktails she'd come up with, retired to the kitchen as Barry and I prepared the fire. It may sound foolish, but I hadn't ever made one in my life, as I had grown up with central heating systems, but Barry was a good, albeit impatient, teacher. I was happy to see that he had recovered quickly from our encounter with Colonel Warton and his German shepherd dog.

Before long, we had a crackling fire going. Luckily, there was still a large supply of wood outside in the shed, so we wouldn't have to worry about it for the rest of the winter.

Then, the door opened and Val appeared in the frame.

"Ladies and gentlecat," Val said triumphantly. "I present to you my newest creation. Winter Spell. Here, have a sip."

She placed two glasses with a bubbling blue liquid on the table next to me.

"Thanks, Val, that's fantastic," I said, reaching for one of the glasses. "Exactly what I needed after a day like this."

"Where's mine, then?" asked Barry indignantly.

Val and I were both taken aback.

"Well… you're a cat, Barry. I don't think you should

take alcohol."

"Oh, what do you think magic's for?" he said. "A temporary stomach-altering spell will do nicely for this evening. Quite simple. Invented it myself, in fact."

"You invented a spell just so that you could booze up as a cat?" I asked in astonishment.

"Well, why not? A warlock is entitled to a drink once in a while, isn't he? Transformed or not."

"OK, Barry, on your little cat's head be it," Val said, leaving for the kitchen once again.

She returned shortly with a third drink.

Of course, Barry had exaggerated the incantation's simplicity. It took me the best part of twenty minutes just to master the complex hand motion, which had to flow in exactly the correct angles and reach precisely a specific point when I had uttered the spell.

"Venter durus," I said for what felt like the fiftieth time.

Something had changed now, however. I felt a tingling in my wand hand that I hadn't before. Barry briefly rubbed his stomach with his paw and then seemed satisfied. We lifted our glasses and were just about to take our first sips when there was a tap on the window outside. It was so dark that we couldn't see anything. Val held her breath. While Barry craned his neck to get a better look.

"Did you hear that?" Val said.

"Yes," I said.

My heart was thumping fast. Who would be calling this late at night? Surely, it wasn't Colonel Warton. At least, I hoped he hadn't followed us here.

I got up from my chair and inched towards the window, grabbing one of the lit candlesticks for light. Beyond the panes, I could make out a burly figure of a man. He was evidently alone. It wasn't the Colonel. But although we outnumbered the man outside, I felt oddly vulnerable. I made a mental note of learning some defensive spells first thing the following morning.

CHAPTER 9

I reached for the latch of the window and pulled. The cold winter air immediately rushed into the warm room. And a familiar voice spoke.

"Hello, hello," PC Bowler said brusquely. "Don't even have a doorbell, do you? You young hippies really are the limit."

"PC Bowler," I said, not bothering to hide my lack of enthusiasm to see him. "It's rather late. Is there something important?"

By the light of the candle, I could see that his face was growing red like a balloon.

"Important? You taking the mickey? Believe me, I have better things to do than barging around houses without doorbells, you know!"

"Right, well, do you want to come in?" I said.

"No, that won't be necessary for what I have to say to you, Missy. I have a busy schedule, you know."

I took a deep breath, trying hard not to blow my top. I knew he only called me 'Missy' because it annoyed me, so I tried to ignore it.

"So what is your message, then?" I asked.

"It has come to my attention," PC Bowler said self-importantly. "That you have been harassing reputable members of the community for no reason at all. I would like to remind you that you are a suspect in a murder investigation. Now that's a very serious business indeed. You'd do well to keep out of any more trouble until the police force can ascertain the guilty party."

"So it was definitely murder?" Val called from behind

me.

PC Bowler's moustache quivered. I could see he was torn between keeping the investigation secret, as he should, and squashing the impudence of somebody questioning his word. After a brief moment, it seemed that the latter impulse had got the better of him.

"Of course it was," he said. "No doubt at all. The only thing left now is to find out how the killer entered the victim's locked room and stole that blooming notebook. Almost like magic, though I have no doubt in my mind that our experts will get to the bottom of it sooner or later. A minor detail in the grand scheme of things, however. Should be settled in no time."

"So who put you up to this?" I asked.

"Up to what?" he said.

"Calling on us."

"Some concerned members of the community who wish to remain anonymous," PC Bowler said importantly. "None of your concern."

"And you still think that I am the guilty party?"

"I cannot comment on current police investigations," he said, brushing a little snow off of his uniform. "But I'd be very careful if I were you. People might think you're trying to cover up something."

"I'm not covering up anything," I said angrily. "If anything, I'm trying to uncover the obvious fact that I'm innocent. And if you'd check the records of the flight Val and I took, maybe you'd come to the same conclusion and stop wasting everybody's time."

"Alright, Missy, I've heard that tale before. No need to repeat it again. All I'm saying is – and this is my final warning – stop pestering the good citizens of Fickleton. We don't need amateurs walking around, pretending to be investigators. That's what we are there for. To do the real investigating, I mean. Leave it to the professionals, Missy."

"And if I don't?" I said.

"Then," he said menacingly. "I will personally make sure that the full force of the law is brought down on you. I mean it. This is my last warning. Stop playing detective."

And with that, he waddled off into the darkness. I had a good mind to bewitch him then and there, but thought better of it. Not least because I didn't know any appropriate spell, though a permanent agreeableness charm might certainly be a start with PC Bowler.

In my anger, I shut the window with so much force that half the pane shot out into the snow.

"Amy, are you OK?" Val asked.

"Yeah, it's just… that PC Bowler gets under my skin."

"Don't worry," Barry said, handing me my wand with his two paws. "We'll get to the bottom of this."

"Yeah, you've got us," Val said.

"Thanks, guys," I said. "Really, I wouldn't know what to do without you. You really are the best."

Barry taught me the spell to fix the glass – which luckily was much easier than his stomach-altering spell – and we resumed our places, drinking Val's excellent cocktails. We spent the next few hours planning our Christmas feast, which would take place a few days after the arts fair in the village.

I had stayed with Val and her parents the previous few years for Christmas, ever since we had become friends in fact. I had no family of my own to return to and had often spent Christmas on my own before. As a result, I hadn't exactly looked forward to the season. But Val's parents had been brilliant. They had treated me as one of their own from the very beginning. It felt like family, almost like it was when I was a child and my parents were still alive. I was very grateful for that experience.

This year, of course, I wouldn't have blamed Val if she had wanted to return home for the festivities. If things had been different, I would certainly have come with her. It wasn't only the police investigation that kept me here. It was the whole atmosphere, the beautiful gardens, this wonderful house that provided seemingly endless rooms and histories to explore. Barry, also, would have had to spend Christmas alone, though I strongly suspected Mrs. Faversham would have at least cooked him a royal breakfast. And of course, there was the little matter of catching a murderous sorcerer that I didn't want to get too far away from. So, I had made up my mind to stay. And Val, being the phenomenal friend that she was, wanted to stay, too.

"We'll just get my parents over for next year," she said. "That'll solve the problem in future. I'll miss them. But you only inherit an estate in the Cotswolds once in your life, eh?"

"I should be so lucky," Barry said, though he was smiling.

"It could have been worse, Barry," I said.

"How come?"

"You could have had someone like Lady Worthington inherit the place," I said. "Just imagine Christmas with her."

"So what do you usually do for Christmas, Barry?" asked Val.

We talked deep into the night with all the different ideas for Christmas spinning in our heads. It felt good to distract ourselves from the case for a while. Val and I had decided to have our cocktail party on Christmas Eve and invite some of the locals over. It was on a short notice, perhaps, but I had a hunch that most of them were so curious about the new inhabitants of Fickleton House that they'd come anyway.

Barry gave off a yawn that indicated it was time to sleep. The fire was almost out by now, with only a few embers left. We said goodnight and made for our rooms, with Barry sleeping in his library as usual. I took a long shower before going to bed, however. I had received quite the shock the first time when there was only icy cold water, but Barry had shown me a crafty spell that made it nice and hot. You simply had to love magic.

***

The next day at breakfast, Barry, Val, and I were sitting at the table while Mrs. Faversham brought in the food. To my surprise, she was followed into the room by Lavalle. I could see that Mrs. Faversham still disapproved of him slightly, though she was perhaps a little less suspicious than the first time.

"Good morning, all," Lavalle said pleasantly, smiling at us as Mrs. Faversham left the room again. "Please, I don't want to disturb you for too long. Just thought I'd keep you up to date."

"Of course," I said. "Please, have a seat. Coffee?"

"Yes, thank you," he said.

There were some spare cups in the cupboard behind us, so I got him one and placed it in front of him on the table. Lavalle looked even more worn out than last time, though somehow it seemed to amplify his dark good looks, giving him a vibe of adventure. He poured himself a generous dose of the black liquid.

"Looks like you've settled in nicely," Lavalle said, gazing around the room.

"Yes," I said. "We'll be staying here for Christmas as well, in fact."

"Oh, you are?" said Lavalle, looking slightly surprised. "Well, there's certainly enough space here for everyone."

Barry was getting fidgety at the table.

"Let's cut the small-talk, shall we?" Barry said, pushing his bowl away from him. "Why are you here, Lavalle?"

"Barry, don't be rude," said Val. "Sorry, Mr. Lavalle."

But Lavalle just laughed, holding up his hands.

"It's alright," he said, inclining his head towards Barry. "You are quite right, of course. And please, it's just Lavalle. Anyway, I've scouted out the area and visited some of the crime scenes already."

"Did you find out anything?" I asked eagerly.

Lavalle shifted uncomfortably in his chair.

"Well, there's still a lot of leg-work to do, of course," said Lavalle evasively. "Nothing definite yet. In fact, I really wanted to know what you're up to."

"What do you mean?" I asked.

"There's word around the village that you've been... asking some pretty pointed questions to certain individuals involved in the murder case," said Lavalle.

"How fast does information travel around here?" Val asked in disbelief.

"If it's gossip," said Lavalle, "I'm afraid it's close to the speed of light. And the villagers are pretty sensitive about this entire business, you know. They're worrying about the arts fair, you see. Trying to keep things as quiet as possible until it's over. Desperate to avoid any sort of scandal."

"Well, PC Bowler's the wrong man, then," I said. "He's the only bull I know who takes his china shop with him."

"Yes," said Lavalle, laughing. "He is rather foolish. Agreed."

"He came round here yesterday evening," Val said.

"Did he?" said Lavalle. "Interesting. What did he say?"

"Oh, the usual tosh about me being a prime suspect," I said. "But they're still looking for the victim's notebook apparently."

"I see," Lavalle said.

"At least they're right to do so," said Barry. "Information on the killer is bound to be in there."

"I think it might be Colonel Warton," said Val

thoughtfully.

"Colonel Warton?" asked Lavalle. "You've talked to him, too?"

"Yeah," said Val. "He acted weird when we mentioned the notebook. He definitely knows something."

"Right," said Lavalle. "Thanks for the pointer. I'll start investigating him immediately, then."

"I don't think he'll be very forthcoming with information, though," I said. "He's the suspicious type. Paranoid even."

"Perhaps a closer look at his house might be in order?" said Barry solemnly.

"Good idea. I'll go there tonight," said Lavalle, taking a final sip of coffee and getting to his feet.

"We can help," said Val. "We've already found out a lot and..."

But Lavalle held up his hand.

"Look, I'm very grateful to you for what you've done. But this really is a matter for the MLE. So please, I beg you, no more solo investigations, alright?"

"People keep telling us that," said Val.

"But you'll come back and let us know if anything develops, right?" I said.

"Of course," said Lavalle. "Especially if there's such good coffee and, if you'll forgive me for saying so, such charming company. I don't think I could resist. Good day, all."

And with that, he left the room. Val looked at me with a peculiar grin on her face, while Barry appeared to be close to bursting point.

"I think he likes you," Val said to me, barely hiding her knowing grin.

"Nonsense," I said. "He meant all of us."

"He was looking at you, Amy," Val said. "And you know it."

"Young cockerel," Barry said dismissively. "All he has to do is put some honey in his words and you both start melting."

"We're not melting," I said indignantly.

"Of course you are," said Barry. "Lapping up every word he says."

"You're just jealous, Barry," I said.

"I don't trust him, that's all," he said. "What do we know about him? It could be him for all we know."

"You sound like Colonel Warton," I said, laughing. "He's an MLE agent, remember? He's on our side."

Barry puffed and protested but couldn't think of an adequate response.

"Fine, fine. But he isn't the sharpest tool in the shed. He didn't even think of going to the Colonel, did he? We found that out on our own."

"He wasn't even in town, Barry," I said. "Leave him be."

I didn't even know why I was defending Lavalle, but Barry was obviously just annoyed at the lack of attention. I had to put my foot down at some point.

"Aaanyway," said Val, trying to change the subject. "Lavalle's going to take over now. We've still got Christmas to prepare for. We haven't got anything in the house, no decoration and no snacks either. And we still need presents, too. Plus all the ingredients for my cocktails."

***

Val was right of course. I was by no means willing to let the case drop, as I was far too curious by nature as well as unwilling to leave my fate to the likes of PC Bowler, but I agreed to a short hiatus until we had properly prepared for the upcoming festivities. I wanted to take the bus into Gloucester, the nearest city, but Val and Barry both insisted on asking Tom. Taking a taxi for such a long distance seemed overly wasteful, even decadent to me, but the obvious convenience was a factor I couldn't dismiss, at least until I bought my own car, which I was determined to do first thing in the new year.

We spent the entire day happily browsing shop windows, buying gifts for each other, and even visiting the enormous cathedral in the afternoon. It might sound strange, yet sitting in cafés always gave me an itchy feeling, as if there was work I was neglecting. I suppose that's what being a waitress did to you after a couple of years. So Barry, Val, and I decided to get takeaway coffees instead. It appeared that Barry's special spell also worked for coffee, with some minor modifications, so that he could sneak an occasional sip when nobody was looking. That went mostly unnoticed, except for when an elderly lady saw me help Barry drink and muttered something about animal cruelty. Under normal circumstances, I suppose I would have agreed with her.

Barry couldn't buy presents himself, of course, so Val and I took it in turns to go shopping with him. Barry sat on my shoulder to get a better view of the items on sale, as well as preventing anyone from stepping on him. In the city, however, few people seemed to care. Barry and I got Val an entire cocktail mixing set plus handbook (with lots of space for the addition of her own recipes). While Barry and Val were out shopping together, I arranged to have a Christmas tree delivered directly to Fickleton House. According to Barry, there were still quite a lot of Christmas tree decorations left from my late great-aunt, so we decided to use them instead of buying new ones. It would both suit the traditional style of the house, in addition to being a way of paying our respects to her.

Finally, we got into Tom's cab and drove home, buried beneath endless piles of parcels and mountains of boxes. I'd never bought so many things in my life. Though I felt a little guilty for doing so, it was a relief that – for the first time in my life – I didn't have to worry about the credit card bill at the end of the month. We spent most of the ride talking to Tom, whose own plans for Christmas involved having his sister over for lunch.

When we arrived back at Fickleton House, it was already dark. I had bought several power banks for our phones in order to circumvent the lack of electricity, at least as a short-term measure. Barry had explained the reason for my great-aunt's disapproval of it, as electricity interfered greatly with magic. As both Val and I didn't want to live completely without it, however, we'd have to find some sort of long-term compromise. For the time being, though, the power banks – to be recharged at Mrs. Faversham's house – would have to suffice.

After dinner, we settled down in the small sitting room at the back of the house as we had done the previous night. It was quickly becoming my favourite room – save for my bedroom upstairs and Barry's library perhaps – due to the fact that it heated up very quickly with a roaring fire and was exceptionally cosy.

Now, with the fire burning next to us, Barry was reading a 16th century magical treatise, wearing old-fashioned spectacles he said he needed for the small print. Val had settled down with a good mystery book she had found in one of the spare bedrooms, while I was content with gazing into the warm flames dancing in the hearth.

Suddenly, there was rap of knuckles on the window, the glass of which I had only mended yesterday with my wand.

"Oh no, not again," I moaned, grabbing the candle next to me. "It can't be PC Bowler."

But it wasn't. The figure outside was much slimmer and taller. I opened the window, shining the light of my candle into the newcomer's face. To my surprise, it was Lavalle.

"Lavalle, what are you doing here?" I asked.

"An emergency. Sorry to bother you like this. But there was no other way to reach you. It's freezing out here, d'you mind if I come in?"

"Of course not," I said, lending him a hand as he stepped over the window sill. "What's wrong?"

He looked at me long and hard.

"I've just come from the village. There's been another development. Colonel Warton has been killed."

CHAPTER 10

We were all stunned by the news. We had seen him alive and, at least under the circumstances, reasonably well. To hear that he had been killed seemed inconceivable.

"But… but how?" Val said.

"He was killed by his own dogs," Lavalle said.

"But that's not possible," I said. "I saw the dogs for myself. They were absolutely devoted to him. To a fault almost. I mean, they would have ripped poor Barry apart if they hadn't been. And us as well probably. But Colonel Warton? No way."

"My thinking exactly," said Lavalle.

"So you're saying he was murdered?" said Val. "But how? I mean, you can't control the dogs, unless…"

"Unless you're a powerful sorcerer," said Barry, taking off his spectacles with both of his paws. "Canines are particularly tricky to hex due to their loyalty to their masters. But it can and has been done before."

"Indeed," said Lavalle. "As you can see, our worst suspicions have been confirmed. My own investigations in the area haven't got me very far, I'm afraid, but they did reveal one thing. Art thieves have been particularly active in the Cotswolds in the last couple of months. The murders I investigated were all wealthy businessmen or landed gentry. All in possession of fine pieces of art that went missing after their deaths. It was all quite cleverly done. The heb police didn't even suspect robbery as the primary motive. You see, they staged the killings as targeted murders, often for other reasons."

"So, you mean the thefts were covered up by the murders?" I asked.

"Precisely," said Lavalle. "Curious, I know. But it makes

sense from their perspective. If they can cover up or at least delay investigations into the robbery while the police are focussed on the murder, the pieces in question will be a lot harder to track. Time is usually of the essence."

"Hold on," I said. "I've just remembered something. The landlord told me that Lady Worthington's arts fair will be featuring a real Van Gogh painting as their main attraction."

"Do you think they could be after the painting?" Barry asked Lavalle.

"It certainly is a strong possibility," Lavalle said. "In fact, I would say it is our best bet. If I can catch whoever is doing this red-handed..."

"You mean *we*, surely," said Barry.

Both Val and I looked astonished. After all, it had been Barry who had been opposed to getting involved in the first place.

"This is a matter for Magical Law Enforcement," said Lavalle. "I told you so this morning. We can't involve civilians."

"But isn't it true that – under Section 24c – MLE may enlist the help of magical citizens in the case of an emergency, even to detain suspects?" said Barry smartly.

Now it was Lavalle's turn to look grumpy for a change.

"A pity you're so well educated," he said. "Yes, it is true. I merely wanted to... protect the ladies."

"We're not just 'the ladies', we don't need protection," Val said immediately. "We want in, don't we, Amy?"

"I think you're outnumbered, Lavalle," I said, grinning.

"This isn't a democratic decision," he said stiffly. "However, under the circumstances, it's perfectly true that this investigation is a lot more complex than one single person can manage. A fact that MLE headquarters admits but does very little about, of course. And it's not as if you hadn't been poking your noses everywhere as it is. I suppose you know too much already not to be properly involved. Probably best if I keep an eye on you. Therefore, I will officially ask you to aid MLE operations during the arts fair."

Barry looked satisfied. Val and I high-fived.

"Please," he said sternly. "This is serious. You will have to follow my orders from now on. To the letter."

"Of course, officer," Val said.

"Whatever you say, sir," I said.

"Addressing me as 'Lavalle' will suffice," he said.

We giggled as he attempted to retain some of his authority.

"Now then," he said, folding his hands behind his head, "tell me all you know about the case. And I want to hear everything. No detail must be spared. It might turn out to be important."

We told him about the various encounters we had had in the previous days, how we had first visited the pub and talked to the landlord, the covert questioning of Lady Worthington and Ethel's evidence against her alibi. Then we recounted our visit to Colonel Warton, and finally our trip to the golf club run by Reynolds, as well as our second meeting in the woods with Colonel Warton on our way home.

"So," I said, summing up. "We've got one suspect down – that's the Colonel – and two left, Lady Worthington and Derek Reynolds. Both with motives. And both have shaky alibis. It must be one of them."

"I'm afraid it's not quite as simple as that," said Barry. "Patricia – that's the girlfriend of Reynolds – also has a strong motive. Jealousy. Reynolds was having an affair with the journalist. She could have followed him to the pub that night after their quarrel and killed the journalist after he left."

"So we have three suspects so far," Lavalle said. "What about the pub owner? Charlie, you said his name was?"

"Yes," I said. "Well, I don't know about him. He

seemed very nice to me, but maybe that was just a front. I mean, he certainly had the best opportunity of all. Remember, her notebook went missing. I'm sure she would have filled it with incriminating evidence, so the murderer stole it."

"Did you find the notebook in Colonel Warton's house?" I asked Lavalle.

He shook his head sadly.

"Not a trace. I didn't have much time, though. Those dogs were making a hell of a racket. Totally mad, if you ask me. Alerted the entire neighbourhood. It was only a matter of time before the heb police arrived, so I left."

"So, whoever killed Colonel Warton also stole the notebook?" said Val.

"That seems to be the most likely conclusion," said Barry.

"Yes," Lavalle said. "Do we have any other leads?"

"We could always speak to Patricia – Reynolds's girlfriend," said Val.

"I don't think that's going to work, somehow," I said. "She's too loyal to Reynolds. For all we know, she might have been the one who called PC Bowler on us. Despite what Reynolds did, she loves him. I don't think she'll give us any information, especially if it might incriminate him somehow."

"But who else is there?" asked Val.

"Well," I said, slowly. "There is one more. Lady Worthington."

"But she won't talk to us, surely?" said Val.

"No, but Ethel will," I said. "Lady Worthington's maid."

"What about her?" asked Lavalle.

"She was willing to talk, even though she was dead scared of her boss. She said that Lady Worthington's alibi was in fact not true."

"Then we should get in touch with her," said Lavalle. "As quickly as possible. This sorcerer is ruthless. Colonel

Warton's death has shown that. But I've got to make sure. I know this is rather irregular, but since you're in on the investigation, I thought I'd ask anyway. Would it be alright to put me up for a few nights?"

"No problem," I said, though Barry looked disapprovingly around the room. "We have enough rooms in this place."

"Excellent," said Lavalle. "Tomorrow night, I'll see if I can find out anything else about Colonel Warton's death. Perhaps even track down that notebook you were speaking of."

"And we'll talk to Ethel, won't we?" said Val eagerly.

"Yes," I said. "But we'll have to get her on her own somehow. Because if Lady Worthington is our killer, we don't want to arouse her suspicion."

***

Getting hold of Ethel wasn't as straightforward as it sounded. We didn't want Lady Worthington to get overly suspicious if she heard we had been asking a lot of questions in the village about Ethel. We didn't even know whether she lived at Worthington Manor or had her own flat somewhere. And time was running out.

An idea came to me the following morning when Val and I were browsing the local charity shop for clothes. Several post offices had evidently gifted the shop some of their old delivery jackets.

"Look, Val," I said. "This is perfect."

"That's awful, Amy. You don't want to wear that thing for the arts fair, believe me."

"No, no," I said impatiently. "Don't you see? We can disguise ourselves as postmen. We can at least get access to Ethel without arousing too much suspicion."

"But these things are ancient. We'll look like time-travelling postmen from the 1970s."

"It'll have to do, Val. At least to fool them from afar. Come on. Or do you have a better idea?"

It turned out she didn't, so we bought the jackets anyway, along with a couple of black shoes and trousers to match them. We slipped them into our bags and headed for Worthington Manor. We decided to walk this time, as calling Tom would have meant that our movements could be easily tracked if someone were to inquire.

Although it wasn't as far from the village as it had been from Fickleton House, it took us the best part of an hour to get there. Once more, we saw the familiar golden lions perched on either side of the gate. We crept into the bushes – well out of sight of the camera – and changed into our post officers' uniforms.

"I look fat in this," Val said.

"I'm sure I don't look too hot either, Val. It'll only be a few minutes."

We rang the bell and a metallic voice answered.

"Worthington Manor."

"Erm, special delivery."

"Right. Back entrance, please."

There was a buzzing sound as the gates were opened for us. We walked up the path to the manor, though this time following the path to the back of the house where I assumed we were supposed to go to.

A sombre-looking man in a butler's outfit was already awaiting us.

"I haven't seen you before," he said with suspicion in his voice.

"No, we're just filling in for a colleague," I made up. "Bad case of the flu."

"Strange mail bags you have, I must say. What is the post office coming to these days?" he said.

Val threw me a told-you-so look.

"Hand me the mail, then, please," the butler said. "My time is precious, and Lady Worthington is already waiting."

"Sorry, it's a special delivery."

"For whom?"

It was at that moment that I noticed that I didn't even know Ethel's last name. Different measures were evidently called for. But I had come prepared.

"Hold on," I said, trying to buy time as I fumbled for my wand in my handbag. "I've got it here somewhere."

"What on earth…" he began as he saw me draw my wand.

"Gratus!"

His eyes briefly unfocussed, and his frown was immediately replaced by a benign smile.

"We would like to give Ethel her mail now. Can you get her for us?" I said.

"Of course, madam," he said blankly and disappeared into the house at once.

"That was close," I said. "Being a witch definitely has its perks."

"Yeah," said Val. "He was really suspicious. Lucky you acted quickly or he would have thrown the door in our faces. Why couldn't we have just done that in the first place, though? Could've saved us from dressing in these silly clothes."

"No, we can't risk being spotted from afar. It may not fool anyone in close quarters but it'll do if Lady Worthington or her husband happen to look out of the window."

Then, the door opened and Ethel appeared. She looked as worried and timid as ever.

"The butler said there was a delivery for me?" she said.

"Hello, Ethel," I said. "This is Mrs. Merryweather. Do you remember me?"

"But…"

"I know I look different, I disguised myself the first time. I wanted to talk to you again. About Lady Worthington. You said she wasn't home when the journalist was killed in the pub and…"

Ethel's eyes grew wide, her breathing shallow.

"I – I can't. N-not anymore. You don't understand. This will get me in all sorts of trouble. Lady Worthington, s-she was really angry at me. And so was Sir Henry. I don't think I ought…"

"Ethel. Please listen. There's been another murder. Colonel Warton was killed last night."

"What? A-are you the police?"

"No," I said. "But we're investigating the case. And we need your help to prevent more murders."

She gulped but finally nodded.

"Alright, I'll help you. But I can't speak now. Lady Worthington would kill me if she found out. Meet me in the village – tonight."

"Alright, Ethel," I said. "Where exactly?"

"Meet me in the pub's carpark – at the back – at midnight. I should be able to get out of here by then without anyone seeing me."

"We'll be there, Ethel," I said. "You're doing the right thing."

***

We spent the remaining hours with Barry at Fickleton House. Lavalle was also there, working. We had put him up in the old guest room in the corridor next to Barry's library. It had been the best room by far, but Barry had not been happy about him sleeping there.

"He snores," Barry said indignantly. "He distracted me from my work all night. I want that man out of the house at once."

"We can't just throw him out, Barry," I said. "We're in on the investigation. He's officially asked us for help."

"And we can officially ask him to leave, too," Barry said. "Really, MLE agents at Fickleton House. Whatever next?"

"D'you want to know what I think, Barry?" Val said.

"Not really, but go on," he said.

"I think you feel threatened by Lavalle," she said shrewdly.

"Threatened? Me?" Barry exclaimed, as if it were the most preposterous idea ever presented to him. "Out of the question. That young whippersnapper is barely out of the academy, barely out of his nappies for that matter. What could he possibly have on me?"

"Well, he's handsome," Val said, flashing a sideward grin at me. "Though not as furry as you, of course, Barry."

"Well," he spluttered, not knowing what to say. "Perhaps I prefer being the only man in the house. I don't see anything wrong with that. He's simply distracting you, that's all."

"You'll always be our number one, Barry, don't worry," I said, tongue in cheek. "Come on, we'd better prepare for our meeting with Ethel. Barry, we need you, too."

"Oh, won't Prince Charming himself bother to come along?" said Barry.

"No, he said he wanted to go to Colonel Warton's house again. You know, to try and track down that notebook. It's absolutely vital to the case."

He sighed as though it was a tremendous burden, though I could see he was pleased he would be coming along and Lavalle wouldn't.

It was strange thinking about Lavalle in those terms. But Val was right, of course. He was handsome. He took himself a little too seriously perhaps, but that was probably normal in his line of work. Looks alone, however, had never been as important to me as to Val. Not that she was superficial. She needed as deep a connection with human beings as any of us. But she certainly was a more visual person than I was, especially in the beginning. And she warmed up to men a lot faster than I did. It was odd but I always felt slow to trust. I had to get used to the idea first, on my own. But, with a curious pang in the region of my stomach, something told me that I was getting used to it a little too fast with Lavalle.

***

At five minutes past midnight, Barry, Val, and I stood in the pub's car park down in the village, shivering despite our thick coats. It was after closing hours for the pub, so only very few cars – including Tom's cab – were still here. Then I remembered that the very first time we came to Fickleton he had said he lived near the pub.

Ethel was late. I had brought my wand with me, just in case, tucked tightly into my inside pocket. I didn't really expect anything to happen, though you never knew. If Lady Worthington had found out that Ethel had arranged a meeting with us, she would have surely done everything in her power to stop her. Whether that entailed murder was another question, of course. One that I intended to find out eventually.

"I'm freezing," Val said.

"I'm not surprised," Barry said. "You only fell into the snow twice."

"Well, it's dark," she said. "I can't see so well when it's like this, even with the snow. I wish Ethel would hurry up."

"Strange that she picked this place to meet, though," I said. "I mean, it's off the main street, but it's pretty exposed to all the houses around here."

We waited another ten minutes without any sign of her. I was just about to say that we had better get back to Fickleton House when we spotted a small car pulling up to us. It stopped in the empty spot next to us, and Ethel got out of the driver's seat.

"Sorry I'm late," said Ethel, sounding out of breath. "I almost had a terrible car crash on the road just a few minutes ago."

"Are you alright?" Val asked.

"Yes. I was really lucky. My heart's still pounding. Anyway, I'm here now. So, what do you want to know?"

"Do you know where Lady Worthington went on the night the journalist was murdered?" I asked.

"Not exactly," Ethel said, looking around the car park as if to check that we really weren't being overheard. "I just heard a conversation between Sir Henry and her the morning after. They were talking about the arts fair."

She hesitated.

"You promise you will keep all of this to yourself?" she asked nervously.

"I promise," I said. "We just want to know who killed the journalist and Colonel Warton. Please, go on."

"Well," Ethel said. "I know it's wrong to eavesdrop but I – there have been a lot of strange things happening at Worthington Manor, you have to understand. Most of the staff are involved, as far as I can tell."

"Involved in what?" asked Val.

"It has something to do with art. Stolen art, if I'm not mistaken."

Val and I exchanged an excited look. We were finally getting closer to some answers.

"For the arts fair?" I asked.

"N-not entirely," she said nervously. "I think it's a lot more than that. They wouldn't dare place them all on display, of course. Lady Worthington is a collector, you have to understand. Sir Henry, too, but he's interested in antique musical instruments mostly. They have a huge arts collection in their basement, locked away. Very few people are allowed in there. It costs a lot of money, too, something they quarrel about all the time. I mean, they're rich, but even for them many of these works aren't affordable."

"And so they buy stolen art since the thieves are usually willing to sell it for a lot less money?" I said.

"Exactly," said Ethel. "That's what they call a 'bargain'.

It took me quite a while to understand what they meant by that. Anyway, on the night that… that poor woman died, Lady Worthington was out of the house. I knew because she always wants me to bring her a tea right before she goes to bed. She didn't that night, so I went to see whether she was there, but her bedroom was empty. And the next morning, she wouldn't tell Sir Henry where she had been. They had an argument, but she just wouldn't tell him. And that's strange, since they usually discuss all of their 'bargains' with one another."

"So you think she was up to something that even her husband would disapprove of?" I said.

"Yes," she said.

At that moment, there was a strange rustling sound, as though a tree had suddenly shook off all of its leaves. Yet there wasn't a single tree in the car park, notwithstanding a small hedge nearby. It was probably just an animal, I told myself, a stray dog or something like that. Barry, too, was quite unnerved and gave me a sharp look, clearly telling me to get to the point.

"Do you know who else might be involved? Someone from the village perhaps?" I asked.

Ethel rubbed her cheek with her right hand as if to soothe herself.

"I don't want to be walking around pointing the finger," she said.

"Please, Ethel," I said. "It might be important."

"Well, there is a man…" she said slowly, nervously bobbing to and fro on the spot. "I've never seen him up close, so I can't be sure whether it's who I think it is. But he's been to the house a few times. At the back entrance, the same way you came earlier today."

"Ethel, what was his name?" I said, steadying her by the shoulders.

She was just about to open her mouth when there was a flash of red light, like a beam out of a powerful laser.

Ethel's body suddenly became limp and heavy and collapsed into my arms.

CHAPTER 11

Val screamed. I let Ethel down quickly behind her car and felt her pulse.

"She's dead," I said, horrified.

"The killing curse," Barry said. "Quickly, after him."

I looked around wildly to see where the beam had come from. A man in a thick, dark overcoat was running towards the main street at top speed. He was holding something in his left hand which could only have been a wand. This was the sorcerer we had been looking for.

We sprinted after him, Barry at the front, as fast as we could. We reached the main street in a matter of seconds, but the man was no longer to be seen. The street was deserted.

"He's gone," I said, lowering my wand. "How could he have disappeared so quickly?"

"By magic, of course," said Barry dully.

"Oh, right," I said.

"What shall we do now?" Val said desperately.

"We need to get an ambulance. Perhaps they can do something for her," I said. "And then the police."

***

The ambulance took Ethel away. According to Barry, the chances of reversing the killing curse were zero, but it was important to let things proceed as normal. We sent Barry up to Fickleton House to tell Lavalle what had happened. The police arrived shortly after. And PC Bowler, who had arrived a little later, was making a real meal of it.

"Caught at the scene of the crime!" he bellowed.

"I wasn't caught," I said irritably. "I called the police

myself."

"Only a clever ruse to put us off the scent, no doubt," he said.

PC Bowler turned to one of his assistants.

"Take down this woman's story, will you?"

"I already have, sir."

"Oh, I see. Doctor's report?" PC Bowler grunted.

"Inconclusive, sir. Looks like heart failure so far. No external wounds, no injuries."

"But that's impossible," he said, gasping for breath as if someone had taken away his favourite toy. "Is that *all* you got me out of bed for?"

"I'm afraid so, sir."

Scowling intensely, he turned around to us.

"Alright, Missy. You might have somehow tricked the experts, but you're not fooling me. I know you're mixed up in this and I'm going to get to the bottom of this if it's the last thing I do."

"May we go now?" Val asked. "It's really cold."

"Alright, alright. You can go. Don't leave town."

"We certainly won't, constable. We'll see you at the fair," I said mockingly.

PC Bowler didn't answer but simply narrowed his eyes in utter contempt.

***

Half an hour later, we had all congregated in Lavalle's room, where he already had a fire burning. Val had made some of her favourite cocktails and we were all sipping at them in a contemplative mood, glad to be out of the cold and beside the warm fire but still shocked by what had happened.

"Poor Ethel," Val was saying. "And she was so close to telling us who had visited Lady Worthington's house."

"And she didn't tell you who it was?" Lavalle asked in

frustration for what felt like the hundredth time.

"No," said Val. "We told you, he killed her before she could say his name."

"At least we know he is male, though," I said. "That should cut our suspects down in half."

"It could still be an accomplice," said Barry, taking a sip from his gigantic magicarita. "If he visited Lady Worthington regularly, she is almost certain to be the head of the operation. In other words, we're looking for someone for delivery. Or perhaps a thief."

"Hold on," I said. "We've never thought of Tom before."

"What, the taxi driver?" asked Val.

"Yes."

"But… that's ridiculous," she said.

"Is it, though?" I said. "He can go pretty much anywhere he wants and just say he took a customer or something. He can park in all sorts of places without people getting suspicious."

"True," said Barry, warming to the idea. "He could be their delivery man. Ingenious. I doubt the police would ever stop him in that old-fashioned cab of his. Just doesn't fit the picture of a smuggler."

"Perhaps," said Lavalle, brushing his hair back with his right hand. "But it's still all speculation. We need solid evidence, especially in a court of magic. They won't stand for mere hypotheses."

"So what do you think we ought to do?" said Barry aggressively.

"Unless we uncover some more evidence, there's only one thing we can do," Lavalle said, pondering the issue. "We'll have to be ready at the arts fair. I'm sure that that is where our killer will strike next. And Lady Worthington has a real Van Gogh on show."

***

In the days leading up to the arts fair, Barry and I spent a lot of time upstairs in his study, practicing jinxes and counter-curses. You couldn't be too careful in preparing for the worst. And we were most likely going to face a most formidable sorcerer very soon. He had proven once already before our very eyes that he was willing to use the killing curse if he had to. And I didn't want to take any chances.

Val, meanwhile, had adapted very well to her psychic abilities. The day at the golf club had proven that she was now able to endure groups of people again, at least for a limited time. She would focus on the psychic angle, trying to isolate suspects and feel their emotions. Since we only had a lot of conjecture so far, her insights would be invaluable. Barry had promised to help her practice on the last day.

Barry himself would be our general lookout and spy. Luckily, I had already acquired somewhat of a reputation as a 'cat person' in the village, since I took Barry almost everywhere I went. I hoped that this apparent eccentricity would come in handy now, since fewer people would object to his presence. And unlike Val and me, he was free to roam around, keeping an eye on everything.

Lavalle, of course, was also going to be there. His MLE superiors had finally sent him some backup. It was none other than his older brother from the organised crime department, Alec. Despite our increasingly friendly conversations, I still had the feeling that he was holding back somewhat. Perhaps he didn't quite trust us yet – understandable in his profession. Or perhaps he was just cagey by nature, used to operating entirely on his own.

On the night before the arts fair, however, I thought I got a glimpse behind the mask. Barry was off downstairs helping Val, so Lavalle volunteered to practice jinxes with me. I was getting quite good at some of them, like the leg-locker hex that I thought might be useful in our attempts to apprehend the sorcerer. Others continued to elude me. What had seemed so easy after my first successes as a witch had radically changed. It was if I had climbed a hill only to find out that the mountains stretched on as far as the eye could see. A little dispiriting, to say the least.

Lavalle himself was an excellent teacher and clearly a gifted warlock as well. He had no trouble conjuring up shields to block my jinxes and hexes, though my disarming charms got through quite often.

"So strange," he said. "I don't usually fall for those."

"Must be the witch who's casting it," I said.

"Maybe," he said.

"Lavalle…"

"Please, Amanda, just call me Rick. That's what my friends call me."

"Do you do this often, Rick?" I asked.

"What?"

"Sleep at girls' houses during your investigations."

"It's not only girls in this place. Barry lives here, too," he said.

"Right you are again, detective."

Rick looked me straight in the eyes. His were a beautiful brown, like the fallen autumn leaves outside that were now covered with snow. Somehow, I hadn't noticed them like this before. And then, he leaned in closer to me, his face almost touching mine. I could smell his shaving lotion. But I stepped back, placing a hand on his chest.

"Please, Rick. This is all so sudden. I – a girl died. I-I just can't…"

"Of course, I understand," he said. "Don't worry."

He checked his watch.

"We'd better get some sleep. The fair starts early tomorrow."

"Yeah," I said, walking over to the door. "Goodnight, Rick. And thank you. For everything."

CHAPTER 12

On the day of the arts fair, Val, Barry, and I walked down together to the village. Rick – though I still called him Lavalle in front of the others for simplicity's sake – said he still had to prepare and would join us a little later. I had my wand tucked away safely in my handbag as usual. Extra training with Barry and Lavalle had certainly helped, but I still felt awfully unprepared somehow.

Once we arrived in the village community centre where the fair was to be conducted, it became instantly apparent that Lady Worthington had left no stone unturned in her attempt to make this an event to be remembered for a long time.

From the garlands decorating the various doorframes to the fresh flowers on the tables, everything was perfect. Refreshments and snacks were available at every corner, and the place was buzzing with volunteers, artists, and visitors from all across the country.

I came across Tom, the taxi driver, in the entrance area. Val had gone ahead with Barry for some refreshments. Tom was standing beside an elderly lady in a wheelchair.

"Oh, hello there," he said in a friendly manner. "Nice that you showed up. Though I must say I can't make heads nor tails of some of these things. This is Mrs. Wallis, by the way, one of my customers. I don't know whether you've met."

"How do you do?" I said.

"Do we know each other?" the elderly lady asked in a rather loud voice.

"I don't believe so," I said, raising my voice to match hers. "I'm Amanda."

She smiled in a slightly senile way.

"Good. I've got a nice picture, you know," she said.

"Oh, she doesn't need to see that," said Tom. "She's only just arrived."

"No, no," she said, rummaging in her handbag. "Here it is."

It was about the size of a palm, a beautiful carving of a man and a woman, embracing.

"A bit naughty," she said, giggling.

"Times have changed, Mrs. Wallis," he said, then turned to me. "Mrs. Wallis bought this picture from one of the local artists. He's upstairs right now, in fact. Excellent stuff."

"Yes, it looks good," I agreed.

Tom leant in a little closer so that nobody would overhear us.

"And between you and me," he said, indicating the carving in Mrs. Wallis's hand. "This is much better than most of the modern rubbish they call art in here."

"I see you've got yourself a picture, too," I said, pointing to the wrapped canvas leaning against the wall behind him.

"Yes, it's a surprise for my wife. A present for her birthday next week. She couldn't come today unfortunately. I promised to get her something."

"I see," I said.

I wasn't quite sure whether I believed him or not. It was all conjecture so far, of course, yet Tom *was* perhaps in the best position to smuggle art for Lady Worthington. I made a note of finding Val and asking her to try and find out what he was feeling.

As I browsed the various works of art on display, I had to admit that Tom had a point in regard to his reluctance to some of the pieces of art on display. Some were interesting, though others eluded me completely. I could simply never shake the feeling that there was an attempt to make something more meaningful than it actually was, to imbue it with the label of art without really deserving it.

I wasn't here, however, to judge the art, I told myself. I kept my eyes open at all times, trying to register every suspicious movement. Many of the village regulars were present, as well as all of our remaining suspects.

Across the room, Reynolds and his girlfriend were apparently entranced by the art, though I strongly suspected that Reynolds was really here to be seen and, if possible, find a few more investors for his projects. His girlfriend Patricia was looking as stunning as ever by his side.

PC Bowler, in plain clothes, was also present. He looked strangely deflated, as if the lack of a uniform had sucked all the authority out of him. He was gazing long and hard at a home-made collection of pottery, frequently nodding his head at an item or shaking it at another.

Over in a remote corner, all by himself, I spotted the pub's landlord Charlie. He was deep in thought, staring at a painting that featured nothing more than two black lines and a red spot in the middle. I didn't want to disturb him, so I moved along, taking note all the same. After I had passed him, I wondered whether he had really been so entranced by the painting. It could just as well have been a clever ruse or even a form of meditation before a heist.

Of course, we were all waiting for the big moment when Lady Worthington was to reveal the Van Gogh painting. Currently, a large white sheet had been used to cover it from sight, adding to the mystery of it all. We had Barry check on it in frequent intervals, however, to see whether it was still there. To do this, he snuck underneath the sheet. Tom's wrapped package had made me suspicious, so I wanted to know whether the picture might have been removed beforehand. But every time Barry returned to us, he reported the same thing. The painting was still there; all was well.

Rick Lavalle had also arrived by now. My heart gave an involuntary jolt as I saw him enter, as if I had missed a step. He smiled at me and, as if controlled by some alien force, I returned it immediately. I felt silly though strangely elated at the same time. There was another man with him whom I didn't recognise.

"Hello Amanda," Lavalle said, after he had steered us to a deserted corner where we could talk more freely. "Valerie's already met him. We've just arrived. This is my brother Alec, from London. He's a private investigator attached to the organised crime department of the MLE."

The newcomer reached out an extremely gnarled hand, undoubtedly the result of many encounters with sorcerers.

"Nice to meet you," Alec said, shaking my hand firmly though without crushing it.

His voice was even deeper than Rick's, though it felt oddly reassuring as well. In looks, the family relation was certainly there, though with pointed differences. Alec kept his hair short in contrast to his brother's longer hair. He had a rugged look to him. All in all, he favoured practicality over Rick's smartness.

"Welcome to Fickleton," I said, smiling.

"Nice place," said Alec. "Are the suspects all accounted for?"

"Yes," I said. "We've seen all of them."

"Good," said Alec. "Now all we do is wait for the big moment. Might take a while."

Rick Lavalle looked strangely nervous around his brother. His gait had lost some of its spring, and he smiled less openly. I wondered whether they had quarrelled before. And sure enough, Rick excused himself, and went in the direction of the bathrooms.

"You know my brother well?" Alec asked me.

"Only a few days really," I said. "Since he's been on the case."

"Yes," Alec said. "He was rather eager to take it. Not really like him but I guess we all get excited for a case once in a while. Didn't even want me here to help out."

He chuckled.

"He… he didn't?" I said, bewildered.

"No. But don't be too hard on him. He doesn't like his older brother meddling, you see."

"But why not?" I asked. "The more wands the better, isn't that what's important?"

"Sure," he said, shrugging his shoulders. "But more wands also mean less credit. Good old Rick, he always was a career man. I always preferred freedom myself. Anyway, I don't mind. I'm doing the department a favour. If you want to remain a private eye in this business, you've got to keep the *Association* happy. And looks like you can use all the wands you can get. This sorcerer seems pretty vicious."

"Yes, he is," I said, thinking of poor Ethel again. "I'm glad you're here, Alec."

At that moment, Val came over to us.

"Hi, Amy. So you two've finally met?"

"That's right," I said. "Any news?"

Val shook her head.

"Nothing. Barry's been prowling around but he hasn't spotted anything so far either. I've talked to Reynolds briefly, Charlie, and the girl from the bakery. "

"Let's just keep our eyes open," said Alec. "You never know in this line of work. Might turn out to be someone you had never suspected before. Sometimes, you just get carried away."

"And what if nothing happens today?" Val asked.

"We'll find another approach," he said.

"The suspense is killing me," said Val nervously.

"You'll be fine. Just focus on what you've got to do," said Alec.

"Yeah, Val, I met Tom in the lobby," I said. "You could check on him if you like."

But then a gong sounded from the main room. It was time for the Van Gogh to be revealed. And so, finally, we all congregated around it. Lady Worthington, dressed in a magnificent silk dress all in white and black, gave a speech on the importance of Van Gogh. How he had been an inspiration to her from her formative years onwards and continued to be so until this very day.

In an imperial gesture, she beckoned one of the volunteers to step forward, evidently to remove the white cover when the time was right. The audience inched closer to get a better look. As they did so, the atmosphere in the room changed dramatically within a matter of seconds. Someone dimmed the lights in the room. People were craning their necks to get a better look, to see the real Van Gogh from as close as possible. Barry skidded towards us, his little paws constantly losing their footing on the slippery floor, but was almost trampled by the many feet surrounding us. I hastily lifted him up, placing him on my shoulder like a parrot so that he could get a better look.

"Did you check?" I whispered to Barry.

"Yes," he said softly. "Three minutes ago. All fine."

I could see Alec, who had positioned himself a little further away, in the direction of the exit. But Rick was nowhere to be seen.

"And so," Lady Worthington said at last. "It is with my greatest pleasure that I reveal to you 'Poppy Flowers' by Vincent Van Gogh!"

There was a great expression of surprise from the crowd but it died down almost instantly. The silence was so absolute that you could have heard a cat purring from fifty yards away. And then, Lady Worthington nodded. The volunteer gripped the white cover and, with a flourish, pulled it off.

But something had gone horribly wrong. There was no Van Gogh.

"It's just a white canvas," somebody from the crowd exclaimed.

Some people began to laugh, though others looked worried. Val and I looked at each other, horrified. Someone had stolen the painting from right under our noses.

"It's gone," Barry said. "That's impossible. I checked it right before she began her speech. That's simply impossible."

"We've got to find out who-"

Suddenly, there was a scream from outside. As fast as we could, we raced outside. Val, Alec, and Barry were sprinting alongside me. We skidded across the floor and reached the exit.

Mrs. Wallis, sitting in her wheelchair, was shaking uncontrollably. Tom, standing next to her, was trying to calm her down.

"Where is he?" I asked.

"Out there," Tom said, pointing. "In the car park. Your friend is already on his tails. Now, now, Mrs. Wallis, it's going to be alright…I'm going to take you home now."

Running full-speed across the car park was Rick Lavalle.

"Who is he chasing?" Val panted, squinting.

"It's Reynolds!" I exclaimed. "Quickly, we've got to help him."

Reynolds, dressed in his trademark white suit, was running towards his car at top speed. A picture with grey wrapping was pinned under his arm.

"He has the picture," I said. "Stop him!"

Alec Lavalle drew his wand at the same moment as I did. We didn't dare throw our jinxes, however, for Rick was far too close to Reynolds.

In a last desperate effort, Reynolds had reached his car and started the engine, pressing the accelerator so hard that his tires screeched as he pulled out of his parking spot.

"Look out, Rick," I yelled.

Reynolds scraped him with his left mirror, painfully hitting Rick on the thigh. He yelled in pain, now drawing his own wand and firing a hex wildly at the car.

But it was too late. Reynolds had already pulled onto the main street and was speeding off in the direction of the golf club. Rick fired another hex, which simply bumped off of the car's windscreen this time.

"Are you alright?" Val asked, as we approached him.

But Rick Lavalle, a fire burning in him that I hadn't seen before, wasn't listening. He turned around to the nearest vehicle, which happened to be a motorcycle, and pointed his wand at it.

"Initium," he bellowed.

The motorcycle immediately sprang to life. He jumped on it and roared onto the main road, in pursuit of Reynolds.

"Quickly, we need transport," said Alec.

I was about to point my wand at the nearest car, when he stopped me.

"We can't risk it, too many hebs."

"But your own brother…" I spluttered.

"… is crazy. We can't do it. Look."

He was right. Almost everyone from the fair had spilled out into the open to see what had happened. I turned around wildly. Tom was still calming Mrs. Wallis down. I quickly approached him.

"Tom, sorry, but can we have your car?" I asked.

"What?" he said.

"We need to catch the thief. It's Reynolds. He's got the Van Gogh. Please, we need to borrow your car."

"If… if you must, I…" he said, bewildered, fumbling for his keys. "Don't crash it, I love that car."

"We won't, I promise. Thanks, Tom."

We rushed over to where Tom had parked his cab. Hastily, I unlocked it.

"You sure you want to drive?" Alec asked.

"Yes," I said, though I hadn't driven for quite a while.

"OK," he said, getting into the passenger seat.

Val and Barry got into the back seat and I put the car into gear.

The roads were icy, and the car kept slipping away. The snow outside and the fact that we were all breathing fast didn't help either. The screens were so foggy I could hardly see what was in front of the car. Rick Lavalle must have been crazy to take a motorcycle in this weather, I thought.

"Where do you think Reynolds is headed?" Val asked.

"I don't know, but this is the road to the golf club," I said.

"Surely he wouldn't go home first?" said Barry disbelievingly.

"He might," said Alec in his deep baritone. "If he's prepared his escape properly."

I drove as fast as I dared on the icy roads for a few more minutes, with no sign of Reynolds's sports car or Rick and his motorcycle.

It turned out that Alec was quite right. When we were close to the golf club, we saw a large private helicopter on the pad next to the main entrance. That could only mean one thing: Reynolds had planned this all along. He was making his escape in the helicopter.

"Look, it's Lavalle's – sorry," said Val, with a glance at Alec. "I mean Rick's motorcycle. But where are they?"

I quickly parked the car on the side of the road. Suddenly, we heard the unmistakable noise that someone had started the helicopter. Reynolds was evidently already inside. We sped over as quickly as we could. And then we saw them. Reynolds and Rick were in the helicopter, fighting over the controls. It was looking bad for Rick, for Reynolds had the strength of a desperate man. Finally, Reynolds managed to kick Rick out of the door, slamming it closed behind him.

"Stop him," yelled Rick, as both Alec and I drew our wands.

I shot a hex at it, but narrowly missed. Alec landed a jinx, but again, as with the car, it simply bounced off the windscreen. He cursed loudly.

"Reynolds put a spell-repelling charm on it," he said. "We can't do anything."

The helicopter was already lifting off of the ground,

gaining altitude quickly. Reynolds was at the controls, his eyes bulging. He looked utterly crazed. The grey package was safely in his lap. He pulled up the helicopter, its propellers fighting violently against the ice-cold winds.

Rick, meanwhile, was back on his feet.

"My wand, where's my wand?" he screamed.

He found it seconds later in the snow nearby. He wasn't taking his defeat lightly, looking almost as mad as Reynolds did in the helicopter. He shot a few curses after it, but it was too far away by now. Next to me in the snow, there was another wand. This had to be the one that Reynolds used. I pocketed it for safe-keeping. At least Reynolds wouldn't be able to deal too much damage until he got another one.

"Rick," his brother said, forcing him to lower his wand. "You can't stop him now. It's over."

"No," Rick yelled, firing another curse into the air.

"Rick," his brother bellowed.

Rick seemed to coming to his senses again. He looked crushed, heart-broken even. And something within me, something compassionate, shifted. It was unbearable to see him in pain. After all our hard work, we didn't deserve this. Rick didn't deserve this.

"Look over there," Val said suddenly. "The helicopter. It's not... flying properly..."

We all swerved our heads, watching the now distant helicopter in the sky. Val was right. The propeller sounds were stuttering and Reynolds was apparently losing control of the machine. Then, the propellers died completely.

"It's dropping like a rock," I said, horrified.

Val closed her eyes as the helicopter dropped into the field below, exploding immediately on impact. Reynolds was dead. And the picture was lost.

CHAPTER 13

Thirty minutes later, PC Bowler was massaging his bushy moustache, taking notes. He hadn't even noticed the robbery and was the last person to have come out of the community centre. He was back in uniform now, however, and in full swing. We had made a full report – as far as it was possible without mentioning magic – to various officers of the police several times now.

"Well," PC Bowler said pompously. "That wraps it up then. Open and shut case. That lets you off the hook nicely, doesn't it, Missy?"

"Stop calling me that," I said irritably.

"It's over now. Lucky for you. I was just about to check on your plane ticket. But it doesn't matter now. We've got the guilty party. And we won't even need a trial."

"Are you finished?" I asked.

"Now, now. You can't rush the pursuit of justice. But I think we have all the information we need. Just for the records, anyway."

At that moment, PC Bowler's assistant – the one who had also been at the pub's car park – arrived.

"Yes, what is it?" PC Bowler demanded.

"They've recovered the body, sir," the young assistant said.

"Good, anything else?"

"They found the picture, too. Burnt almost to a crisp, sir. But some of the frame is still recognisable."

"Ah, well," PC Bowler said. "Can't have it all. Alright, lets wrap it up. You can go now, too, Missy."

***

An hour later, Val, Barry, Rick Lavalle, and I were once again sitting in front of a blazing fire in Fickleton House. Alec Lavalle had gone back to London again, though he had given me his card in case I needed to get in touch with him at short notice. Somehow, with the way the case had turned out, I didn't think so, but it was good to have it all the same.

Mrs. Faversham had made an excellent dinner, and nobody felt like moving very much after the events of the day. Rick would be staying one last night, a fact even Barry was too exhausted to complain about. Despite the food and the warmth, there was a distinct atmosphere of disappointment.

"That's it then," I said gloomily. "The painting's lost. And so is Reynolds. He won't be able to testify."

"Yes," Lavalle said. "But at least it's over now. We can all go back to our lives. He won't be able to harm anyone anymore."

"But he can't tell us anything about the art smuggling ring," I said.

"Is Lady Worthington going to get away with it, do you think?" Val asked Lavalle.

"No. I've been in contact with my superiors. They're going to ransack the place first thing tomorrow morning."

"That's what I don't understand, though," I said. "Why would Reynolds steal the painting from Lady Worthington? I mean, I thought they were in on the whole smuggling business together."

"Maybe Reynolds got tired of playing second fiddle?" said Lavalle. "Who knows. What matters is that we got the killer."

"What was he thinking anyway, taking the helicopter in that sort of weather?" Val asked.

"That has been bothering me, too," Barry said. "A sorcerer wouldn't have needed to do any of this. Why drive if you can take a broom and fly? Much safer."

"Maybe he didn't have a broom?" Val said.

"Plan an art heist of this kind and rely on heb transportation? Highly unlikely," said Barry.

"He was crazy, alright," said Lavalle. "Almost killed me with this thing."

He held up Reynolds's wand, the one I had found next to the helicopter pad.

"It was lucky you came out of there alive," said Val, nodding.

"Yes," said Lavalle. "I figured that I'd stand a better chance in a fist fight, so I went for him. Seems I was wrong. If only I had got him out of that helicopter…"

"You can't blame yourself," I said. "He was barking mad. He had the power of ten men."

"Yes," said Barry. "I've rarely seen someone so talented."

"That's high praise coming from you, Barry," said Val.

"It is," he said with no trace of false modesty. "And those spell-repelling charms he created on the car were exceptional. They're very difficult to pull off since they have to scale with the spell that hits them. And they get weaker with every successive hit. In other words, the cumulative protective force must be stronger than the energy that hits it."

"What shall we do with his wand, then?" I asked. "The one Reynolds dropped, I mean."

"Oh, I'll hand it over to the department," said Lavalle. "They collect these things, you know. Even if they're not needed for a trial."

"Will there be a hearing?" Barry asked.

"A brief one, I suspect," said Lavalle. "Just to wrap things up. Well, I suppose I'd better get an early night's sleep. Got to get up early in the morning. I've got Tom coming round to pick me up."

"Aren't you travelling the warlock way?" asked Barry.

"What's the warlock way?" I asked, bewildered.

"Flying by broom, of course," he said.

"The department insisted I use heb transportation," said Lavalle.

"It's a pity you can't stay longer," said Val.

I could see Barry silently protesting in the background. He had not enjoyed the disturbance that Lavalle had brought to the house. I was sorry to see him go, though a part of me was glad. I didn't think I could get involved with anyone right now, not even with Rick Lavalle. The events had shaken me up more than I liked to admit.

"Well, I'd better turn in," Lavalle said again. "Good night all."

We all wished him goodnight. I thought about going to bed myself but knew I wouldn't be able to sleep anyway. It was only 8 o'clock, after all. It looked as though Val and Barry felt quite the same way. The case, as PC Bowler had so clearly expressed, was open and shut. The culprit, Reynolds, had been caught. And yet, however much I tried, I just couldn't put it out of my mind.

"Something's not right about this case," I said broodingly, breaking a long silence.

"Yeah, Reynolds certainly was a maniac," said Val, yawning.

"No, no. I mean, there's something that keeps bothering me. I can't put my finger on it but…"

"Oh, Amy, just let go," said Val. "It's over."

Perhaps she was right. I tried focussing my brain on something else. Barry, Val, and I continued to sit there for I don't know how long. But I just wasn't able to shake the feeling that something was seriously wrong. And I had to get to the bottom of it. I had to make sure.

"I'm going out," I said suddenly.

"What, now?" Barry exclaimed.

"Yes," I said simply.

"Where are you going, Amy?" asked Val, looking a little worried.

"I'll tell you later," I said. "Just… just stay in here. I need to do this alone. I'll be back soon, I promise."

I must have been crazy to do this all on my own. Perhaps I was. But I had to find out whether my hunch was true. I took my coat and headed as quickly as I could through the snow to Mrs. Faversham's house, since she had the nearest phone I could use. I knocked on the front door. Mrs. Faversham appeared in slippers, evidently surprised to see me.

"Why, Miss Sheridan, to what do I owe the pleasure?"

"Sorry to bother you at this time, Mrs. Faversham. I need to make a phone call. Could I borrow your phone for a minute?"

"Why, yes, of course. Dear me, you do look serious. Is anything the matter?" she asked, concern stretched throughout her old face.

"Yes, thank you. I – I just need to make that phone call."

Mrs. Faversham, slightly bewildered, stepped aside. Her phone was an old-fashioned one with a sturdy grip where you still had to turn the wheel to dial.

"Tom's taxi, what can I do for you?" asked the taxi driver's familiar voice on the other end of the line.

"Hello, Tom, this is Amanda Sheridan. I wonder if you're free at the moment? I need to go to the golf club."

"The golf club? Alright. When would you like me to pick you up?"

"Right away, if that's possible," I said. "I'll wait for you at the front."

"Alright," said Tom. "See you in a bit."

***

Twenty minutes later, coat wrapped closely around me against the cold, I got out of Tom's now quite familiar cab in the golf club car park.

"Could you wait for me?" I asked. "It's only going to be a few minutes."

"No problem," he said. "I'm free all night so far."

"Great, thanks," I said.

I hurried over to the main entrance. The receptionist looked at me in a pleasant manner, so I decided to try my luck without a wand first.

"I need to see Patricia…" I began.

"I'm sorry, madam. She has asked not to be disturbed under any circumstances," the receptionist said.

"Fine," I said under my breath.

What had I ever done before to extract information from people, I wondered. I took out my wand and quickly pointed it at her. Less care was needed, as the lobby was almost completely empty.

"Gratus," I said.

"Miss Patricia Redgrave is in the residential suite. Third floor, to your right and at the end of the corridor."

"Thank you," I said.

I headed for the open elevator and pressed the number three. There were hardly any guests around. Perhaps they had heard what had happened and left. Or they had returned home to their families for Christmas.

I reached the third floor and followed the corridor to the residential suite. A light was burning inside. I gently knocked on the door.

"Leave me alone," came the unmistakable voice of Patricia from the other side.

"It's Amanda Sheridan. It's very important."

"I don't' care," she said. "Go away."

"Patricia, I don't believe Derek Reynolds was guilty. I'm here to clear his name."

There was a pause, then a rattling of keys, and the door to the room swung open. Patricia looked a wreck, which was completely understandable, of course.

"What did you just say?" she said, wiping tears from her

eyes.

Her breath smelled strongly of alcohol. And she was evidently having trouble focussing me properly

"I don't think your boyfriend was guilty," I said. "But I need to speak to you to prove it."

"You really mean that?" she asked. "You're not a reporter or… or something like that?"

"I swear," I said.

She stepped aside, allowing me to enter. Judging from the crumpled pillows and bedsheets, Patricia had been in bed before I had knocked. On the nightstand, there was a large bottle of clear vodka. It was half empty. As was to be expected, she had taken the news very badly.

"I – I thought you were the police at first. They called on me. Asked me a lot of stupid questions about… him."

"I'm very sorry for your loss, Patricia," I said. "I believe that there is reason to believe that your boyfriend Derek Reynolds was framed and then murdered."

"W-what?" she asked, staring at me in disbelief.

"He has been accused of stealing pieces of art, now including the Van Gogh from the arts fair, correct?" I asked.

"But I told them it wasn't true," she said, starting to cry. "H-he didn't do any of those things."

"Yes. I think the person who actually committed those crimes killed Derek Reynolds. But I have no proof. It's all conjecture. It's been that way from start to finish."

"What do you want to know?" she said, wiping away her tears again.

"That night – when he went to see the journalist -"

"How did you know that?" she asked, flabbergasted.

"It doesn't matter now. But did he see anyone else there?"

She thought for a while.

"I didn't like speaking about it. He hurt me deeply with what he did. But he was a good man. He tried to set things r-right."

"Yes, but did he see anyone else there?" I asked again.

"I-I wouldn't k-know," she said, though her voice shook as she did so.

"How did you know that he had seen the journalist?" I asked.

"He – he just…"

"You were there, weren't you?" I said. "You followed him that night after you had a row in that Italian restaurant."

She broke down in tears, bobbing uncontrollably to and fro. I laid my arm around here, trying to comfort her. After a few minutes, she felt strong enough to speak again.

"Yes, I followed him. I saw him go into the back of the pub. There's an extra s-staircase there. He didn't want to be seen by anyone in the pub. And I saw him come out again. I waited all that time, hidden in the car park."

"And was there anyone else present?"

"I-I can't remember. I was so upset that he would do such a thing. W-Wait. There was someone. He bumped into Derek on the way out. But it was all very brief. I didn't think about it at the time at all."

"Can you describe this person?"

She nodded.

"I think so."

***

A few minutes later, I was back downstairs in the lobby. There was only one more thing I had to do. There was a payphone at the back, near the restaurant. I took out the business card that Alec Lavalle had given me in case of any developments. I needed him back here as soon as possible.

"Alec Lavalle, PI," he growled into the phone.

"Hello, Alec, this Amanda. Something's come up. Something big. I know it's on a very short notice, but can you come over?"

"Right now?" he said.

"Yes. It can't wait I'm afraid."

He breathed into the phone.

"OK, I'll hop on the broom immediately. Should take me a bit over an hour."

"All the way from London in this weather?"

"I've got a fast broom. I'll meet you at the house," he said and hung up.

I stepped back outside into the snowy cold. Tom was waiting for me, as promised. I got into the cab, which had cooled off quite a bit in the meantime.

"Sorry for taking so long, Tom," I said.

"You've got everything you wanted?" he asked.

"Yes, all fine."

He started the engine and pulled out into the main road.

"Strange affair, wasn't it? At Lady Worthington's arts fair, I mean. I've heard she's still devastated."

"I can imagine," I said. "Is your wife any better?"

"Oh, yes. You know, it was funny. Remember that picture I bought her?"

"Yes, I remember," I said.

"Well, I put it in the car after we were done. Drove home and put it safely in my room. And what do you know? Next day it's gone. Not a trace. I thought at first my wife had got it and was playing a trick on me."

He laughed throatily.

"But she didn't know anything either. Funny, isn't it?"

"Yes," I said. "It certainly is. Who sold you the picture?"

"Oh, a visiting artist, Kessel, I think the name was. Something German. He had his own booth."

"Did you... see him wrap the paper around the picture?"

"Wrap the paper?" he said, sounding slightly perplexed. "As a matter of fact I didn't, come to think of it. He said he needed some paper and had to get it from the storage room. I waited, and when he returned it was already wrapped. Why, is it important somehow?"

"Yes," I said. "I think it's very important. I believe you inadvertently helped our murderer and art thief smuggle Vincent Van Gogh's masterpiece out of the community centre, unnoticed. And when you had unknowingly brought the Van Gogh to the safety of your own home, our thief and murderer broke in and retrieved it. The perfect heist."

"But Mr. Reynolds…" he began.

"… was innocent," I said. "The real killer and thief is still at large. And I think I now know who it is."

CHAPTER 14

Tom dropped me off at Fickleton House. It wouldn't be long before Alec would arrive. I only hoped he wouldn't be too late. Time was of the utmost essence. The snow was falling more heavily than ever. It wouldn't have surprised me if he had been delayed. Fast broom or no fast broom.

I could see the light burning in the sitting room downstairs. It seemed Barry and Val were still up. I let myself in through the front door and closed it behind me. Once more I walked through the long corridors, passing the spot where I had first seen Barry on my very first day here. It was odd that this place had so quickly become a home to me when it often took me months to get used to a new flat. But the house had a personality of its own, with its quirks and its sounds and its history that were unique.

I opened the door to the sitting room. Val had fallen asleep near the fire, which was low but still burning, and Barry was sitting on her lap. He peeked up his head immediately as I entered the room.

"Oh, it's you, Amy. Lavalle is looking for you."

"Alec?" I asked.

"Alec? No, Rick, of course."

"Oh," I said. "What did he want?"

"I don't know," said Barry unhelpfully. "But he went out again."

"What's wrong, Barry? Are you mad at me?" I asked.

"Of course I am. Running off on your own like that. It's stupid, even dangerous."

Val was slowly waking up now.

"Dangerous? Did someone say dangerous?" she said drowsily.

"It was worth it, Barry. I think I know who it is."

139

"What do you mean?" asked Barry. "We know who it was. It was Reynolds."

I quickly explained what had happened, how I had interrogated Patricia. I also told him of Tom's wrapped picture he had bought at the fair.

"You don't mean they smuggled it out using Tom as a courier, do you?" asked Val.

"They used him as an unwitting accomplice, yes. After all, our murderer wanted the picture above all else. And the opportunity was perfect."

"So, this German artist was in on it?" asked Barry, frowning.

"That or he was hexed into helping," I said. "Either way, it was a good way for our killer to stay out of the limelight while making sure he got the picture out safely. He could then easily retrieve it later by breaking into Tom's house. Tom is very talkative. Anyone who took a taxi would have no trouble finding out where he lived or what his routine looked like. Then, it was only a matter of evading his wife at home. And that is exactly what happened."

"But why do it like that?" asked Val. "I still don't understand."

But comprehension was gradually dawning on Barry.

"Yes, brilliant," he said, smacking his paw on the armrest. "If you swapped the Van Gogh for a counterfeit at the right time, it would have taken an art expert to tell the difference. And that is, unfortunately, not one of my qualities. At least not yet."

"Yes, but if you remember, it was a blank canvas when Lady Worthington uncovered it," said Val.

"A simple, timed dissolving charm could have easily done that," said Barry. "Pretty basic magic."

"But why?" asked Val. "Why not leave the counterfeit in plain sight and get out with the picture? It would have taken hours before someone examined the picture more closely and noticed a difference."

"Because that wasn't all our friend was after," I said, pacing the room. "You know what always bothered me about this case? The missing connection to Lady Worthington. She helped traffic the goods and bought a lot of stolen art herself, and yet it was *she* who had in turn been robbed at the arts fair. There had to be a connection, but I didn't understand it until just a few minutes ago. Why, for instance, had Lady Worthington threatened to kill that journalist, Michelle Nosworthy?"

"Probably because she found out something about her stolen art collection," said Val.

"I think," I said, "more specifically it had to do with how it was acquired and redistributed. That information was dangerous. And our murderer was also implicated. He had to remove her as quickly as possible. He couldn't have known, of course, that Patricia Redgrave would see him while she was spying on her boyfriend at the pub. But then an idea must have struck him. He had found out in the meantime about Reynolds's affair and was determined to pin the whole thing on him."

"Who else knew about the affair, though?" asked Val.

"I'll get there in a minute, Val. Just imagine, you can get the Van Gogh, free of any inquiry because the perpetrator has been killed and the painting unfortunately perished in the flames of that helicopter. Quite convenient, don't you think?"

"You mean the whole thing was staged?" said Barry.

"That's right," I said.

"But who staged it?" asked Val.

"Well, can't you think of anyone?" I asked. "Who knew of Reynolds's affair? We found that out. Who knew Colonel Warton acted in a suspicious manner in regard to the notebook and thought he might have it in his possession? We did."

"And shortly after he was killed, with no notebook to be found…" said Barry, his face darkening.

"Exactly," I said.

"But that's ridiculous, Amy," said Val. "It can't have been any of us three."

"It wasn't," I said. "Which leaves only one person who could have possibly done it."

"Rick Lavalle," Barry breathed.

At that moment, the door behind us gently swung open. It was Rick, holding a wand in his hand. He was wearing a curious smile on his face.

"Well done, Amanda," he said quietly. "I'd clap for you, but I prefer to keep this wand pointed at you at all times."

"*You* are the sorcerer," said Barry, jumping from Val's lap onto the floor. "*You* killed those people."

"A masterpiece, was it not?" he said.

"But why?" said Val.

But I thought I already knew.

"He told us right at the beginning, Val," I said. "He said that sorcerers don't need to steal money, they can simply conjure it up. But you can't do that with real art. It's unique."

"Precisely," said Lavalle, his lips curling into an evil smirk.

"How long have you been in the art-smuggling business?" I demanded. "Are you even a real MLE agent?"

"Oh, yes," he said. "Yes, I still have my badge if that's what you mean. A rather tiresome job I had often thought of leaving behind me. Until I came across Lady Worthington. She had quite the network going, you know. She was a heb, but all the more useful to me. I worked for her for a while, getting to know the important contacts."

"But Michelle Nosworthy had found out about it, hadn't she?" I said.

"Yes," he said, his face contorting into a look of hatred. "She was about to expose me and the entire network. I couldn't let her do that. I had to silence her."

"But the notebook was gone," I said. "And that's where

she had put all her information."

"Clever girl," said Rick Lavalle. "Yes, it was gone when I arrived. Someone must have taken it just seconds earlier. I must say, I was very grateful to you when you told me about Colonel Warton. And you were right, of course. He had stolen it. I searched his place and found the notebook. Naturally, he had read the whole thing, so I had to make sure the paranoid old fool couldn't tell anyone."

"So you bewitched his own dogs to kill him," I said grimly. "You evil…"

"Oh, but you mustn't be sensitive about these things, Amanda," Rick Lavalle said, laughing. "It's the daring and the flawless execution of the plan that really matter. Just think of how close you were to finding out my identity when you met Ethel in the car park. My timing was perfect. A masterpiece of crime. Unique even, you might say. Like a work of art."

"I should have known you were no good after Ethel died," I said. "No normal person would have made advances after something like that had happened. Only a psychopath would."

"Ah, well," he said. "That is your definition of 'normal', not mine. In any case, I have no interest in *being* normal. Would anyone but an exceptional sorcerer have carried out the plan at the arts fair? How I switched the pictures so that good old Tom could carry the real Van Gogh out for me? And even in the unlikely event that they caught him, there was no way of tying it back to me."

"And you needed a scapegoat," said Barry angrily. "So you blamed it on an innocent person."

"You say innocent, yet I think you would have seen it quite differently if you had read what Miss Nosworthy had to say about Reynolds and his shady business dealings. But yes, I needed someone to take the blame. Reynolds was the perfect target since you already suspected him. The heb police would also be satisfied. I bewitched the car to repel jinxes just in case. And then, I waited for my plan to unfold. I placed a control charm on Reynolds while you were all watching Lady Worthington and gave him a wrapped canvas that roughly fit the size of the real Van Gogh. I made him flee the premises and tore after him just at the right moment, for all the world to see what a dutiful MLE agent I was."

"And you took the motorcycle so that we wouldn't be able to follow," said Val.

"Quite right. I needed time. Time to prepare to kill Reynolds. He was still under my control, though the distance made it difficult. We nearly crashed multiple times on the road. But we managed to get to the golf club. I made the helicopter spell-repellent and dropped a spare wand in the snow for you to find. You were so desperate for clues, after all. So I decided to provide you with one."

I heard a faint thud in the snow outside, but Lavalle wasn't paying any attention.

"The heb police bought the whole thing immediately, of course," Lavalle continued. "Few people liked Reynolds. And they were glad to wrap the whole thing up. And now, the real Van Gogh is mine. But it isn't going to end here. Lady Worthington has many more masterpieces of art in her cellar. And the good thing is that she won't be able to go to the police when they're gone. That's where I'll be going tonight, in fact. As you can see, it is the perfect crime."

"Not quite so perfect," I said. "We found you out."

"A slight error," he said casually. "One I intend to correct immediately, however. You were a little too curious for your own good. But as they say, curiosity killed the cat. Say goodbye, Amanda Sheridan. It was nice knowing you. A pity we didn't kiss."

He raised his wand, pointing it directly at my heart in preparation for the killing curse. But at that moment, Barry catapulted himself forward, lodging his razor-sharp teeth into Rick Lavalle's thigh. The latter cried out in pain, while the red beam of his curse missed me by inches as his arm jerked upwards. Val and I reacted at once. We hurled ourselves on him, while Barry bit his hand until he relinquished hold of the wand.

And then, the door to the room opened once more. Finally, Alec Lavalle, drenched from head to toe, had arrived. He was wearing a grim face as he saw the scene before him. He pointed his wand at his own brother.

"That's enough, Rick," he bellowed. "Rick! Let them go."

But all three of us, plus Barry, were wrestling relentlessly on the floor. Despite our numbers, Rick was gaining the upper hand. Alec lowered his wand and blasted us apart, making me hit the wall with a painful smack. Rick, sensing his chance, desperately clambered for his own wand which was only a few inches away, but Val kicked it just in time as Rick bent down to retrieve it, sending the wand flying to the other side of the room. Rick Lavalle tore after it on all fours.

"Catena!" boomed Alec's voice.

His wand emitted a long, heavy chain that quickly wrapped itself around Rick, who skidded to a stop on the floor, unable to move another inch.

"That's better," Alec growled. "Now, what's going on?"

And then, we told him the entire story. Alec stood there, face growing paler and paler. Even for him, it was hard to believe that his own brother was responsible for such heinous crimes.

"Alec," Rick pleaded, struggling against his bindings. "They're lying. It's all nonsense. It was Reynolds."

"I've heard enough, Rick. You're coming with me."

"But... but you're my brother," said Rick.

Alec merely looked at him in disgust.

"Enough," he said.

Then, Alec turned to me.

145

"I'll take him straight to London. I'll let you know when we arrive. You take care of yourself now."

"We will. Thank you, Alec."

Alec opened the door. His brother Rick looked daggers at me as he tried to get up, but he stumbled and fell each time. Alec raised his wand once more and levitated his brother through the door and into the corridor. Alec nodded one last time to us. And then, they were gone.

For a few minutes, we were lost for words, until Val finally gave me a long and hard hug.

"You've solved it, Amy," Val said, beaming. "You did it!"

"We all did, Val," I said, beaming back.

"Hey, what about the picture?" said Val suddenly. "The Van Gogh, it must be…"

"Let's check Rick's room," said Barry.

***

And sure enough, as we scoured through his things upstairs, opposite Barry's library, we found the Van Gogh, safe and sound, carefully wrapped in grey paper. We found the journalist's notebook, too, though some of its pages had been ripped out – probably by Colonel Warton in the attempt to destroy the information that Michelle Nosworthy had gathered on him.

"Remind me to send this to Alec in London," I said. "I'm sure they can apprehend Lady Worthington with this information. As well as strengthen the case against Rick Lavalle."

"You know, I always had a bad feeling about that bloke," said Barry, stroking his whiskers in a self-congratulating manner.

"Alright Barry, you *were* right. Happy?" I said, laughing.

"Not quite," he said. "You promised me that cocktail party. It's Christmas Eve tomorrow, after all."

CHAPTER 15

Two days later, on Christmas day, I still couldn't believe what Rick Lavalle had done. With all the preparation for the cocktail party, there seemed to have been some sort of delay in realisation. I was too busy to really think about it, I suppose. Or perhaps I just preferred to *be* busy so I wouldn't have to. We had been looking for the murderous sorcerer all over the village, except of course within our own walls. And he had played his part like a master, up to the very end.

Barry and Val, though both shaken by events, had recovered much quicker, at least from what I could tell. Barry – sedentary even by feline standards – was glad to be able to get back to his research instead of 'gallivanting across half the country', as he called it. Secretly, I think, he was also glad that justice had been served and that Rick Lavalle would be placed on magical trial in London. Still, the irksome duty of catching the killer had been lifted from his shoulders. Barry was now free to focus his attention on other things again, like perfecting his automatic massage charm for the sofa in his library.

Val was determined to hone her skills as a psychic even further. It had been a shock to her, especially, that she hadn't been able to detect Lavalle's true intentions from the start, though I strongly suspected that even seasoned psychics would have been fooled by him. Barry, as an experienced warlock, didn't seem in the least surprised that she hadn't, though he promised to practice with her more often.

Undoubtedly, Rick Lavalle had had a special knack for affecting and manipulating the people around him. Barry, as I'm sure he would remind us for a very long time to come, had indeed distrusted him from the start, though for more selfish reasons than he now admitted. And it was certainly true that Lavalle had successfully evaded Val's sensors. But psychic or no psychic, I felt it was much worse with me. I had not only *not* suspected him, but I had confided in him, even trusted him. The horrible truth was that he had charmed me. However brief that connection had been, there was no denying it, and I felt sick when I thought about it. How could I have been taken in by a homicidal sorcerer? I'd be wrestling with that question for quite a while, I was sure.

In the meantime, however, it was Christmas. I owed it not only to myself but especially to both Val and Barry to pull myself together. There would be enough time to brood and feel sorry for myself in the new year. I tried to bring myself back to the present. I still had to clear away the cocktail glasses in the sitting room downstairs.

The cocktail party the previous day had been quite the success. Many of the villagers, curious to see Fickleton House and its new inhabitants, had flocked up the hill through the light cover of snow to our doorstep. I recognised most of them from the arts fair, though I had had little time to get to know them properly then. Val had modified her recipe for a White Russian cocktail, so that Barry could slurp it from his bowl as if it were milk. And so, we had spent a long and pleasant evening at Fickleton House. It was our first party here, though I was sure it wouldn't be the last.

Now, however, we had to clean up the considerable mess. I scooped up the remainder of the glasses, placed them all on a tray, and then made for the kitchen. Val was doing the washing up. She had somehow got some hot water going, and the entire room was full of steam and soap bubbles. I was just about to enter the kitchen when I stumbled over something furry and was barely able to keep the tray from crashing to the floor.

"Careful!" came Barry's resentful voice from below me. "You're upsetting the post."

"Sorry, Barry," I said. "Didn't see you there. What on earth…?"

Barry, wearing his reading spectacles, had placed at least two dozen letters on the ground in the corridor, just outside of the kitchen door.

"Barry's been reading the mail for me," said Val. "Thought it'd save some time. We haven't checked it since we got here, you know."

"Oh, right," I said. "Anything for me?"

"Just some letters from the bank, the MLE – full of snivelling apologies no doubt," Barry said, throwing it on the ground in contempt.

He still hadn't forgiven the MLE that the only agent they had sent here had turned out to be the murderer himself. And for once, Val and I wholeheartedly agreed with him. Barry rummaged around in the pile with his paw and retrieved a purple envelope, squinting his eyes to read the tiny yet neat handwriting.

"This one's from the Royal Committee for the Preservation and Restoration of Lighthouses."

"The what?" asked Val over the noise of clunking cutlery and glasses.

"Quite a mouthful," I said. "What do they want?"

Barry smartly slid his claw along the edge of the envelope, producing a folded letter from within.

"What does it say?" I asked curiously.

"Oh, just some tosh about old lighthouses," said Barry dismissively. "Your great-aunt was apparently a member of their committee. And they want you to step in for her. Bunch of lighthouse loonies, if you ask me. Well, one more for the rubbish heap, then."

He threw it onto the pile with the MLE letter.

"Hold on, Barry," I said, picking up the letter.

I quickly scanned it. Judging from the rough paper and

imprints, it had probably been typed on an old-fashioned typewriter. It appeared that my great-aunt had not only been part of the committee but was also one of its founding members. The letter sounded desperate, almost pleading. The Royal Committee for the Preservation and Restoration of Lighthouses had evidently seen better days.

"They're inviting me to attend their annual meeting," I said. "In two months' time."

"Where exactly?" asked Val.

I browsed the contents of the letter again.

"*On a cosy little island off the west coast of Scotland*," I read. "They've got a small hotel there. Doesn't sound too bad."

"You're not actually thinking of going there, are you?" said Barry.

"Why not? It's not like Amy's going to run into another sorcerer there," said Val, laughing. "I mean, that would really be bad luck."

"Exactly," I said. "And you're coming with me, of course. Both of you. We could all do with a little trip. And forget about this… this whole affair."

"I'm in," said Val enthusiastically, taking off her rubber gloves and smacking them down, sending a dried cocktail glass back into the soapy water.

But Barry simply made a series of grumbling noises.

"Oh, come on, Barry," I said. "It's only for a few days."

"The thing I hate most is water," he said darkly. "Right after Scotsmen, that is."

"Barry," said Val. "Don't be a spoilsport."

"*You're* spoiling my research," he said grumpily.

"We won't go if you won't come with us," said Val flatly. "Won't we, Amy?"

"That's right," I said, grinning. "We'll get our own car, Barry. You can take all the research you like along with you. And all the tuna cans we can fit into the boot."

He looked at us for a moment with narrowed eyes.

"Alright, alright," he said finally. "You win."

"We *all* win, Barry," said Val, bending down and affectionately patting him on the head. "It's going to be fun."

"Of course," he said sarcastically. "What could possibly go wrong when we're stuck on a remote island in the middle of nowhere?"

"Well," I said. "We'll just have to find out."

*****

Amy, Val, and Barry return in NO CAT IS AN ISLAND, the second part in the series, available on Amazon.

For even more of Barry, receive a discount for books 1 – 5 in the COZY CONUNDRUMS COLLECTION, available now on Amazon.

DON'T FORGET YOUR FREE BOOK

Thank you for reading CURIOSITY KILLED THE CAT. I hope you enjoyed reading it as much as I did writing it! For updates and your free novella, THE COCKTAIL CONUNDRUM, you can join the free mailing list at writingmysteries.com (it's also known as Barry's fan club – but better not tell him that).

To spread the word, please consider leaving a review on Amazon and on Goodreads. It's a great way of supporting the series. A quick note that you liked it really goes a long way and is deeply appreciated.

I'll see you in the next adventure!

Yours truly,
T.H. Hunter

DEDICATION

To my beloved spouse, who believed in me from the start.

Printed in Great Britain
by Amazon